CW00835619

# Steve Braker

# African Slaver

A William Brody

African Adventure Novella

# African Slaver: Contents

# Foreword

All of the locations in this book exist. I went to great pains to ensure that all distances, longitude, and latitudes were also correct.

The islands, villages, and towns I describe are an actual description of the areas, and the people living in them.

The village is a real place; however, I did take some author's license on the description.

The diving in Pemba is truly excellent. I would advise any of my readers that a trip to Pemba Channel offers a once in a lifetime scuba diving experience. The dives are challenging: up to one hundred and twenty feet of crystal clear water, then you hit the drop off which just plunges into the darkness. I have visited many times; the current is strong sometimes, but all the dives are memorable. If you go to Pemba, make sure you follow all of the safety procedures for a dive.

Spearfishing is a great sport in East Africa and totally legal in Tanzania. I always free dive when I am spearfishing. I believe with scuba tanks the fish really does not stand a chance so any sport is lost!

The three dhows in the story do not exist, but are based on some of the dhows I have sailed and built over the last fifteen years. They are a fantastic way to get around the East African coast. The styles of the dhows do vary as you travel along the coastline, depending on the ocean around the area and the type of work.

The islands of Ziwayu actually do exist exactly where I say they are and how I describe them. There are a quirky group of fishermen who live on these tiny rocks. They dry shark meat as there is an abundance of different shark species just off the coast. It really does stink!

I would like to thank my wife Pauline for encouraging me to write this book. She says I have done the most dangerous things she has ever heard of. I am sure that is just a wife talking to her husband, but when I think back on my ocean adventures with the dhows, the speedboats, the fishing, and diving, all I can think is that I am a very lucky person to have survived the journey and to have lived it!

My second shipmate, Gumbao, was a real person. We sailed the coast from Jewe islands in Tanzania to the tip of Kenya on the Somalian border for many years. He was a great guy; we had some good times together, but unfortunately, he died in 2015. I miss him badly when I am out on the ocean. The two of us could stay on a boat for days, not speaking one word, but always knowing what to do.

I hope you enjoy this novella.

Steve                                                    Braker

# East African Coast

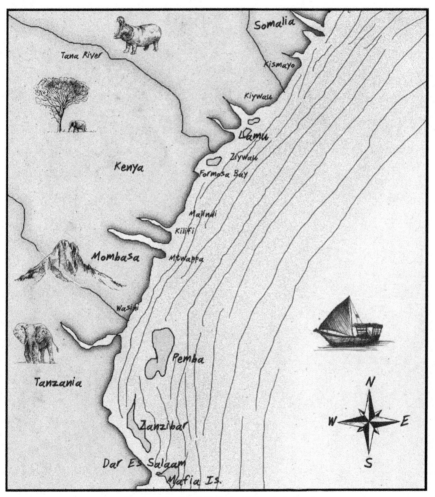

Cover art by J Caleb @ jcalebdesign.com

# Chapter One

Sitting perfectly still, totally relaxed, suspended in space, Brody was 50 feet down, according to the depth gauge strapped to his arm, in crystal clear water, sitting motionless, and waiting. His Rolex Submariner was counting off the seconds; so far one hundred and twenty had slowly ticked past. Freediving is all about relaxing. You stop thinking, sitting in a trance like state, a Buddha hanging serenely in the ocean, holding a six-foot pole with a razor-sharp spear!

His lungs were relaxed and full. Life was all around him in the depths, constant movement and color from every direction. The current was very slightly pushing him to the northeast. His body felt warm even at this depth. He glanced up to monitor his position. Clearly visible above, the small wooden sailing craft was safely anchored to the reef. Earlier he had slipped off the boat, swimming until the bottom disappeared into nothingness. Then, after taking several deep breaths, he duck-dived, finning for a few strokes until the lead weights around his waist started slowly pulling him down.

Hassan was sat on the boat, fiddling with the engine nervously, tidying the ropes and sails, continuously glancing at the place where his new customer had just disappeared. The odd couple had met on the jetty a few days earlier. Hassan had spotted this new 'Muzungu,' a white guy, jumping off the weekly ferry. Hassan approached, with his best tourist grin plastered across his face, and offered to help the newcomer with the dive tanks and other equipment. As usual, this quickly flourished into finding accommodation, and a bite to eat. Hassan usually earned his daily cash catching fish, but Brody had come to dive. The two shook on an agreement. Brody would hire him, and his dhow with the small rusty outboard, on a daily basis until he left the island. This would also give Hassan a regular stable income for his mother, father, and sister, plus himself. The deal sat well with Hassan. It was guaranteed money, a rare thing on the island. He figured he could also do some fishing while his new customer was down below.

Brody's watch was still ticking away the seconds. He had about a minute left. He loved it down here. So silent and peaceful, away from the dreams and memories he fought against daily. His lungs started to tighten. He looked up again to the bottom of the boat; it seemed to be getting further away with every second ticking by, but Brody always wanted to push that little bit more, always one more step. He held on, then took careful aim. The lovely coley coley was swimming in circles about twenty feet away from him, interested in this motionless creature just sitting, not swimming, not moving, not breathing. Brody aimed and fired. The bolt from the spear gun was dead on target, just behind the pectoral fin. It went straight through the fish's heart. Brody's practised aim was proving to be unstoppable here. But the water was crystal clear, he could easily see the bottom another sixty feet below him.

The fish was about 12 pounds, a good size. There were a ton of them living off this reef; this one would not be noticed. Brody believed in freediving for fish as it seemed fairer than using his tanks. At least the fish had some advantages over him in this alien environment.

The coley coley struggled, then went limp. They were known for being the least energetic of the large eating reef fish in tropical oceans. Brody quickly dragged it in, then started for the dhow above.

When his head broke the surface, it was still only 07:00, but the temperature was already nearly 100 degrees. He felt the tropical sun burning his scalp immediately. Paddling to stay afloat, Brody threw the line to Hassan, who gratefully took it and started hauling in the dead fish before the sharks got a scent of it.

Hassan shouted, "Hey, Boss, that was long. I thought you had joined the fish and swam away!"

Hassan always hid his fear that his boss and paymaster would disappear over the side and never come back!

He was a Swahili, the coastal tribe of East Africa, born in the water. They were natural boatmen, and could tell the weather, the wind, and tides before they could walk. They knew the best reefs, fishing spots, mooring points, and the finest of what the tiny town had to offer, which wasn't a great deal!

During their initial meeting, Hassan had taken Brody to a lovely secluded house, or shack depending on the way you looked. It was on an isolated beach and very quiet, with just the wind in the palms, and the waves lapping on the pale white shore. There were no luxuries like electricity. The water came from a well, dug some eighty feet further up the beach, away from the high tide line. The fishing hut was suspended above the water on stilts. The one-room, plus cubicle shower outback, was constructed of cut lengths of bamboo, tied together using twine weaved from coconut leaves. Hung just outside the rickety front door was an ancient, smoke-stained hurricane lamp, and inside was a small cot with a mosquito net slung above. That was about it for amenities. Hassan was not sure if it was what his new customer would like, but he had taken it without a second glance.

Brody did four more dives for fish that morning. He had only wanted one, but knew Hassan would be able to sell them in the market. His family would eat well tonight. Brody also knew the Swahilis were so generous he would get more food than he could eat, cooked by Hassan's mother, so the sentiment was not entirely altruistic.

After the last dive, Hassan coaxed the outboard back into life, which took a while. Brody pulled the big stone anchor off the bottom, and they set off back across the lagoon.

Brody sat on the small wooden deck of the boat, gutting the fish as they slowly headed back towards the village and his new shack. The journey would take about an hour as the outboard had seen much better days, and Hassan was praying over it to last until they reached home. He had gutted so many fish it was second nature; his mind started to wander. He was so lucky to have found this place, a tranquil paradise in the middle of nowhere; he could live peacefully and forget the past he so wanted to lose.

William Brody was born in the UK, in North London on the estates near Wood Green. The place was good enough, an average inner-city suburb, with a large shopping centre or mall to hang out in, and a public school, doctor's office and post office, all the usual stuff. His mother and father both wanted the best for him. His dad worked for the local council, and his mom in an insurance office on the high street. Life was all right, a bit mundane, but OK. Brody enjoyed school, but was not so good at the education part. Sports, especially swimming, was great, but sitting in the classroom was not so much fun. His reports always said that he could do better and must try harder. The inner cities didn't have a lot to offer Brody. Inheriting his father's wild Irish ways, he longed for the outdoors. When the school offered outdoor pursuits or camping, his name was at the top of the list. Every Friday, he would load his bike with camping gear and set off into the evening, not returning until late Sunday night.

Whenever school was too much, he would head down to Canary Wharf on the River Thames and watch the boats go by, smelling the tidal river as it raced in and out. His dream was to join the Merchant or the Royal Navy and sail the seas for the rest of his life; he could think of no better way to spend his days, afloat on the water he loved so much.

On his sixteenth birthday, he applied for the Merchant Navy, but was turned down as his grades in school were frankly rubbish, plus the few scrapes with the law did not help. The next stop was the Royal Navy. The recruiting officer acted the same way.

The Sargent said, "Look, lad, you can go and do better at these exams and come back after a couple of years."

Brody was not happy. He asked out of exasperation, "What else is there?"

The recruiting Sargent looked him up and down, then said, "Well, lad, you look damn fit. What about the Royal Marines?"

He had not thought about them before. It would be at least near or on boats. One second later, the forms were signed, his dad breathed a deep sigh of relief and handed the lad over to the Royal Marines.

With a jolt, Brody was back to the small fishing boat. All the fish had been gutted and were laying at his feet. The boat was only a few minutes from the small jetty. Hassan expertly maneuvered the dhow up against the wooden poles. They landed the five coley coley on the quay, and Hassan immediately found a basket made from coconut fronds. they seemed to use them for everything. He then raced off along the dusty track towards the small fish market. Brody knew Hassan would get a good price for the fresh fish because the local boats had not left before 04:00 this morning, and it was a good eight hours' round trip.

Hassan met his sister along the track, and gave one of the fish to take home to their mother for the feast tonight. Since Brody had landed on the island, the family's fortunes had changed. They were starting to enjoy his company, and the rent from the little house on the beach also helped.

Brody collected his gear and headed off down the beach towards his pad. It would be noon soon. This place would touch 100 degrees Fahrenheit, combined with ninety-five percent humidity. No fans or air conditioning made the situation almost unbearable. His usual pastime during the baking afternoons was to find some shade and slump in a hammock or wander the beach looking for interesting shells. Often, he would meet some local fishermen, sitting on the beach mending nets. Chatting with them was enjoyable. The old men did not have a word of English nor him Swahili, but they were good-natured and happy to have someone with new stories to tell. In the way of travellers meeting for the first time, after a while, and using many hand signals and drawing pictures in the wet sand, everything became clear.

The Marines, then the Special Boat Service had instilled in him the importance of learning the language and culture. Mixing with the locals was second nature. Brody sat and patiently learned one word after the other. Earlier in the week the old men had taught him 'Samaki,' the Swahili word for fish. He was going to use his new word tonight at the meal.

Right now, all he wanted to do was head back to the little house and take a snooze. Freediving was always tiring. The dull ache inside his head was growing as he wandered back along the soft white sands of the beach to the shack.

Although this was a strictly Muslim island, the elders always managed to find a local drink called 'Mnazi' made from fermented coconut juice. When he got to the shack, two old men were sitting on the porch. They had gnarled fingers and hands like tree bark. Once they had been fishermen, but were too old for that hard life now. The two old men spent their days mending nets, sharpening hooks, and telling stories about when the fish were bigger and the ocean was more terrible. They also liked to sneak a drink. With three wives each and who knew how many children, who could blame them! These old reprobates had snuck off and decided Brody's house was a good idea. The plan was to blame the 'Muzungu,' white man, if they got caught.

The 'Mnazi' was sweet like treacle. The old men had three small wooden cups with short hollow sticks for straws poking out of the top. The bottom of the straw had old sailcloth wrapped around the base as a filter. 'Mnazi' came in ancient, battered gourds and was reverently poured equally into each cup. Pieces of coconut husk floated on top of the milky drink. It did not smell so good either, but it was potent. The trick was to hold your nose for the first couple of shots, then the smell seemed to disappear.

The fishermen had a good haul. Brody knew he would drink too much. The sweet, rough liquid was intoxicating. Brody had drunk his fair share of booze over the years. It had caused problems in the service on more than one occasion, but had all been covered up and glossed over as he was a good soldier. But that was then, and this was now. He was his own boss, no demands rules or regulations.

They enjoyed the drink; telling stories in English and Swahili. As the alcohol flowed, he understood the Swahili much better, and them English. After four hours, they were like old friends. All the gourds were scattered on the sand. The team were just formulating the best plan ever, to steal a boat and head for the mainland for more booze. Hassan came trotting down the path towards them. He was horrified that the old guys had made Brody drink, but they didn't care and were falling asleep in the house.

Brody was drunk, slurring his words. Thinking he knew what he was saying, he was speaking to Hassan in Swahili that made no sense. Hassan left them to get his food. The plan had been to invite Brody for dinner with his parents, but as they were strictly Muslims, this would not        be        a        good        idea.

# Chapter Two

**Three Years Ago**

**Kismayo Southern Somalia**

The outboard had been shut down as soon as they heard the small surf on the offshore reef. The team of Special Boat Service operators paddled silently towards the coast, and into the shallow saltwater creek. They knew after four miles there would be a dense mangrove swamp on the southern side of the river. With the NVG's it was easy to see the gnarled roots tunneling deep into the soft mud around them. The trees were supported above the low tide level by these tangled root systems. The slick, slimy mud came up to their knees in some places. It was soft, sticky mud that sucked you into the ground; you could lose a boot easily in this mess if you did not break an ankle or leg trying to negotiate the roots. The small team found a narrow inlet into the mangroves. Using the NVG's they were able to navigate along the inlet, until they found a secluded area to haul the Zodiac up and cover it with the net. Once the craft was camouflaged, it would be invisible to all, but a very keen eye. There had been satellite coverage of the whole area for the last six weeks. It seemed very few people, if any, passed this way. Brody sincerely hoped this was the case, as it was their only way out.

The team had landed 40 miles south of Kismayo three days earlier in the dead of night. This country was so barren it was tough to stay hidden; the ground was rock hard down here in the south, from years of relentless sun. There were no trees to be seen, just a hot and dusty desert. Moving around in the open during the day was dangerous. The horizon was eight miles away and could be sighted in all directions. The four-man team consisted of Captain Brody, Sargent Dave Gillis and two operators. They had served together for the last nine years all over the world, from the sweat boxes of the jungles in Zaire, to the days in Iraq dealing with the fiber optic cables. They were a close team, training, living, and working together. Mark Jones was a Welsh man, tough as they come. He was big for an operator at just short of 6ft, as strong as an ox but still able to blend into any environment, which was so important to the Special Boat Service (SBS) operators. The SBS didn't go for huge guys full of muscles. They wanted to be able to slip into ports and harbors without anyone noticing. In Zaire, the team had lived in the jungles for eight long weeks. They had felt like Henry Stanley, trekking silently through the dense undergrowth day after day, following a gang of known drug smugglers. Finally, being able to corner them and finish the job.

Lastly was Andy, their demolitions man. Every SBS team had to have one. He had been instrumental in many stealth attacks in Kuwait after the invasion. The SBS teams had been sent along the coast to the harbors and inlets to mount small night raids on the supply ships. They had been so successful the Iraqis had reinforced the troops along the coast of Kuwait, taking many of their most valuable soldiers away from the front line.

The sweat was dripping off the ends of their noses. It was dark, the NVG, (Night Vision Goggles) were showing faint signs of movement in the darkness. Brody shifted his legs slightly in the sand to get the blood flowing again.

The distant horizon to the east had a faint glow; he could hear the slow, even lap of the waves in the distance. Sound traveled in this flat, barren landscape; the cocks had started crowing. There early morning movements in the village, the smell of fires being lit, tea being made, goats being let out to find whatever grazing they could.

They all enjoyed each other's company and carried on like English Marines when they could, all joking and horseplay. But Brody knew these men and trusted them with his life. He was aware they were fully committed to the team, that when the chips were down, he could count on them for his life, as he would gladly give his life for them.

The tight-knit team had marched the forty miles from the drop off zone at night, using their NVG's the whole way. It was not safe to move in the barren land during the day. You never knew who was watching. A British Special Boat Service patrol found on Somali soil would be given an automatic death sentence, every team member new it.

The area of Somalia around the Kismayo old port was a stronghold for the Somali Patriotic Movement, the new terrorists of the current era. They had started as a loose bunch of radicals, privates from the local militia, gradually coalescing into a formal movement led by a madman calling himself Sheik Al- Dahabu, 'the golden one'. As the civil war had worn on and the new group did not see the promises that the land would be free and Allah would rule, they had turned to kidnapping, piracy, and drug smuggling. Sheik Al- Dahabu had shown himself to be very adaptable. In his addled mind, a world ruled by Allah's Sharia law was easily combined with murdering innocent sailors or addicting kids to heroin. As long as it was only infidels who suffered and died and, of course, he made a good profit.

It was now 1998. The Peacekeepers and the Americans had left three years ago. The place was a madhouse with militants driving around in Technicals with 30 caliber machine guns attached to the flatbed. They would shoot without hesitation. The Movement, as they were known, applied strict Sharia law: a woman could not be out alone, all must attend the mosque five times a day to remain holy.

This place was dangerous; any mistake would be fatal. They had an extraction to do. If they could pull it off without too many contacts with the SPM, Somali Patriotic Movement, that would be just fine. They also had to plan for the forty-mile return trip which they knew would not be as quiet.

Brody motioned to Dave; he immediately picked the radio, telling command, "We're in position and observing."

14

The four-man specialist team were on the outskirts of Kismayo. Having arrived before dawn, they were now holed up, watching the bullet-ridden walls of the main street. There were craters all around the dirty hovels from mortar fire, and burnt out vehicles sat forlornly, rusting on their rims. A general air of sadness and despair hung over the place like a heavy thunder cloud.

This was Africa, always hurting, always suffering. It saddened Brody, he loved this continent, he had been all over it since he had joined the Marines as a 16-year-old. He was in love with the people, the smells, the beautiful wildness of the place. He especially loved the east coast which is where he had spent his downtime from the service diving, sailing, and just enjoying the atmosphere.

But now was business; the team had an extraction to do, and it had to go smooth and fast.

Their mission was to find Ismaad Ali Kartoum, a preacher in the local mosque. His lectures were all about the Italians stealing their country and corrupting it with western ways, then offering nothing in return. Ali Kartoum would drag up the past, preaching about the Ethiopian barbarian tribes' invasion from the west at the speed of a Landrover. When the attacks had hit the capital Mogadishu, the rich and influential, who sat in the western style coffee shops surrounding the Al Aruba hotel, had fled as one. Within twenty-four hours, the streets were empty of all foreigners, leaving the Somalis to fend for themselves. The Italians had just taken the incredible bounty of Somalia, abandoning the people with nothing but a raging battle-ground which quickly turned into a civil war. This divided the country into three clans controlled segments, constantly fighting among themselves. Ismaad Ali Kartoum blamed the western influences, then the sudden departure or all ex-patriots for the current problems his beloved country was facing.

The Muslim cleric was a dangerous man, a Jihadist wielding considerable power over a wide area with an uneducated population. He needed to be removed. If the western powers did not start to eliminate these people who were spreading hate, and used children as soldiers in a war that had ripped the country apart, it would only get worse; more radicals would appear, making the west a more dangerous place. Where terrorism would most definitely rise.

A tall Somali stooped to come out of one of the small huts. He was lean, well over six feet tall, and carried himself with authority. The man glanced at the goats on the dirt road, then kicked a scrawny chicken out of the way. At that moment, the mosque started singing to the world, *"Allah Akbar! Allah Akbar!"* This was the call to prayer. The tall, lean Somali seemed to look straight at where Brody and his men were hidden in the wadi on the outskirts of the town. He shrugged, then walked on towards the sound of the prayers; the day had begun.

The team had recognized Ali from the photos they carried. They carefully watched him and his militia all day, counting heads, counting weapons and equipment.

All four members of the crack team were experienced in this type of work. Each man carefully assessed possible ingress and egress points, then rally points all around the perimeter. Their years of training took over. Each movement and thought came as second nature to them, total concentration on the job at hand. The operation was planned with meticulous precision. Each man had to know his exact role in the extraction.

At 16:00, when all were at prayer again, Brody decided to advance closer to the houses where they could start to get into position. The plan was to take the village by surprise, bundle up Ali, and get him back to the cruiser waiting for them over the horizon, some twenty-five miles offshore. This would be a silent takedown. Everything would be over before the village realized. Then they would head back to the ship, hand over Ali, and go back to base for some beers.

At 16:30, everything changed. A patrol of two Technicals came over the horizon from the north, trailing a huge plume of dust behind them. The trucks raced into the village, firing off a few rounds from an AK 47's to announce their arrival. These Russian guns were the scourge of Africa. There must be millions of them all over the continent. You could buy them in the markets, some were twenty years old. The machine gun had been built as a utilitarian, multi-use assault weapon. It used 7.62 ammunition, and could get through over 100 rounds per minute on fully automatic in the hands of a seasoned user. These were militia, poorly trained soldiers, so fully automatic was the name of the game.

The new arrivals caused a shift in Brody's thinking. As the Technicals unloaded their human cargo, he noticed the soldiers were short and slim with T-shirts and scruffy shorts. Dave handed him the binos so he could zoom in on the vehicles. There were four short, skinny, malnourished soldiers standing at the front. Each held AKs across their chests, and all wore golden bandanas wrapped around their heads. This sign aligned them with Sheik Al-Dahab. The soldiers looked experienced, but they were still kids no older than 12 years. This meant trouble; child soldiers were very difficult to deal with, especially for a westerner. Trained soldiers had no weapon against women and children. Usually if confronted they would run away, but this group looked like battle-hardened veterans. He had not met a soldier that had an answer for this kind of situation. Your moral code would just not agree with shooting kids.

He decided they would wait until last prayer, then slowly infiltrate the village from the south and the northeast off the beach. The team would split into two groups. One would get to the hut and take Ali quietly. The second would disable two of the Technicals and use the third for a quick getaway. Once the team were back at the mangroves, they would dump it in the creek where it would sink into the deep mud and be lost.

Nightfall came quickly. On the equator, with strict twelve-hour days, one minute there was light, the next was almost pitch dark. Brody's team used the shadows to manoeuvre into their positions around the village. He took Andy, and Dave circled the silent village with Mark; they had practiced this routine a hundred times during exercises, but nothing was like the real thing. Everyone's heart was beating a little faster as the adrenaline started pumping into their veins.

The teams checked their weapons. Each man carried Sig Sauer P226s, the preferred sidearm for the SBS. It was a powerful handgun which used 9mm rounds. Slung across their shoulders were Heckler & Koch G3's. Brody preferred this versatile weapon with the fold-down stock for close-quarter or use in vehicles. It had settings for semi-automatic and fully automatic and was fed from a 20-round magazine. Using the three-shot burst setting, it was a lethal weapon in his experienced hands.

They entered the village at 02:00 hours as agreed. All was quiet. They had comms. Brody was the lead for his tactical team and Dave for the other. The two groups approached the village, moving in the shadows, keeping clear of the moonlit areas, and staying low. The ingress was peaceful as they had expected. No one was being torn from their bed yet.

A mangy dog watched as Dave slowly crept down the main street. It scratched itself then looked at the black-clad figure, with NVG's on its head, then casually wandered off. Brody's team reached the hut they wanted; it was silent inside and out. The moon was waxing, the sky was full of stars, a peaceful night. Brody met Dave at the door. The other two had circled off to immobilize all but one Technical.

Mark and Andy rigged the spare Technicals with plastic explosives on an electronic timer. Andy, as the explosive expert, checked the charges and carried the detonator. If they were real lucky and the mission went as planned, Brody and his team would be able to get a good half kilometre from the village before anyone noticed. They knew once the first Technical started up the village would come out to see what was going on.

Andy and Mark finished rigging the Technicals and set about getting the spare one ready to start. Mark chose the one in what he hoped was the best condition, praying it would start quickly.

They clicked twice on their mics to signal all was set. Brody and Dave moved into position, trying the door of the dark, silent hovel. It was not locked; this was a small village. They had expected as much. Creeping silently into the room, the two apparitions in black noted an elderly woman and a young girl sleeping on a single bed. This was a problem. The SBS operators stealthily moved through the curtain to the second room. Ali was asleep on a cot next to the wall, and a kid was sleeping on the floor.

Brody looked at the peaceful scene. He thought to himself, *"Shit, this could go wrong!"*

Dave used hand signals, motioning Brody to wake Ali with his S.B.S steel dive knife held to the preacher's throat, hoping this would keep him quiet.

Brody woke Ali up with his hand over his mouth, the razor-sharp blade of the combat knife pressing so hard a thin red line appeared the cleric's neck.

Ali woke up with the pressure of a hand on his mouth and a solid cold feeling against his throat. With wide panicked eyes, he laid as still as a statue, frightened to move. This could be anyone. As a preacher of Allah, he had made many enemies.

The two men clad in black motioned with hand signals, slashing their throats, and pointing their weapons at the other occupants of the room. Ali nodded his understanding, his eyes wide with fear. Before he realized who his kidnappers were he was gagged, and plastic fast-lock ties wrapped and tightened around his wrists, trussed up like a chicken.

Brody clicked twice on his coms to signal the other team to prepare for extraction. His mind was racing, planning the next move, looking at options, comparing actions and reactions. But so far so good, now for the tough bit.

The three men slowly started to leave, their feet making no sound on the dirt floor. The air was so thick with tension, it could be cut with a knife. Dave and Brody knew one wrong step, one loud noise and all hell would break loose in seconds. The boy stirred in his slumber, reaching out to clutch his beloved AK47, pulling it in closer to himself; it should have been a play toy not an instrument of death. The two operators and their new captive made it to the door without incident, the old crone blissfully unaware of the new visitors. Brody slowly cracked open the wooden door to sight the dusty lane; the moon was just showing, giving them enough latent light to see the area well through the NVGs.

The street was empty. After shutting the door quietly behind them, Brody took point with Ali just behind him, Dave's G3 pushed into his spine. They hugged the shadows, moving as quickly as possible towards their egress point. Brody clicked twice on the mics to let Mark and Andy know the captive was in possession and they were thirty seconds out.

Brody's eyes flitted from door to door, constantly monitoring the shadows. This might be a trap. Guns could start blazing at any second.

Strangely, so close to death, this was the time he felt most alive. His brain tried constantly to put the mammalian fight or flight instinct into play, but the years of training held it in check. The adrenaline dump in these situations was akin to a high on heroin, the reason so many ex-soldiers ended up as drug addicts, sleeping rough on the streets.

Then they heard it. Up ahead was a shout and a scream, then shots rang out. Mark and Andy's position had been discovered. Brody and Dave acted as one, the years of exercises taking over, in situations like this, everything was reflex and muscle memory. Dave took the six. Brody grabbed Ali by the scruff of the neck and moved as fast as possible to the pick-up point. They raced towards the cars as people came stumbling out of their houses. No Somali leaves home without his weapon; it only took seconds for bullets to start flying.

A man rushed out from one of the huts weapon at the ready. He spotted them immediately and turned to fire, but Brody's round took him in the throat, throwing him back through the entrance into his house. The door behind Dave opened. He grabbed it, slamming it into the guy's head as he poked it out, then pulled the door back open and fired into the room, killing three militia in one automatic burst.

Automatic gunfire was erupting from all over the village. Most seemed undirected and sporadic. But, there were more sustained bursts coming from Mark and Andy's direction: this was going to shit, and Brody knew it. Rounding a corner, they could see Andy and Mark defending a position in one of the vehicles; Mark was twisting wires under the dashboard, Andy was giving covering fire. The Technical burst into life. Andy and Mark jumped into the front cabin, Mark in the driver's seat. Brody was running with Ali, dragging him along, Dave was just behind them keeping pace, firing off short bursts to keep the village at bay. Just maybe the gods were looking down on them today and the team would clear the village. A few more yards and they would make it.

Then everything changed. Brody saw the windscreen of the technical shatter in a hail of bullets from further down the lane. Four militia were flanking them, the kids with the AK's. One stood in the road in front of the Technical, emptying a magazine into the windscreen. Brody saw Mark slump to the side with blood gushing from a head wound; his face was ripped to shreds. Andy screamed, firing at the kid; this was sick! How could you shoot at children? They were just kids, but deadly kids. Their eyes were blank, devoid of humanity, dead in a way. The twelve-year-old went down as Andy emptied his magazine into him, the poor tiny body. He should have been playing football, or running in the park, or, better still, at school.

They reached the car in seconds. Andy bundled Mark's dead body into the back seats of the twin cab. Dave jumped up to take over the 30 caliber on the flatbed, and Brody climbed in, throwing Ali in as well. Just as he was clambering into the driver's seat, he sensed more than felt shots hitting the side of the truck. He spun to face the danger. Three boys were standing in the dusty lane. They were raising their weapons, ready to kill Dave, who was loading the 30 calibre. He would be next in the onslaught of bullets. These were kids for God's sake. He could not shoot kids, it was just wrong. Everything moved in slow motion: he could see Dave up on top, loading the weapon with his back to these young boys.

He could see the village coming alive. He could hear Andy screaming, "Move! Move!" He could see the cold, brown eyes of these three children in front of him as they raised the AK's, he cursed and knew his life was going to change forever. The G3 was in three burst mode. He knew there were 15 rounds left: he watched himself as he let three rounds hit each child, they rocked as the bullets hit them. Their pathetic T-Shirts shredded into pieces as the 7.62 rounds tore their frail young bodies to pieces. He knew his time to reckon with God would be a tough one. He was now a killer of children.

The flatbed roared into life and raced off into the night. A few seconds later they heard the explosions as the other Technicals erupted in flames.

With head-lights off, NVG's on, and the GPS (Global Positioning System) showing the direction, they headed back the forty miles to the hidden zodiac. As soon as the Technical had covered a few miles, silence enveloped the car racing across the desert. It seemed to the team like it had all been a dream. But reality still shone through like a search beam in the night. Ali was tied up, Dave was in the back, keeping an eye out for anyone following them, and Mark was dead.

Brody put it all out of his mind, keeping the mission in focus; they reached the swamp without incident. The Technical was pushed into the creek where it sank into the soft mud. After ten minutes, all that could be seen was the rear bumper. The saltwater would destroy it before anyone found it.

The three-man team, with their captive, and their dead, paddled to the mouth of the creek, then powered up the outboard and headed to the rendezvous point 4 miles offshore where they would be picked up by a larger semi-rigid inflatable then back to the cruiser.

The mission was hailed as a success. A dangerous man had been removed from Somalia, sending a strong clear message to the militia and other growing organizations. Terror would not work against the West.

Brody got a promotion for the mission. Mark's body was sent back to the UK for a full military funeral with honors. He had died on a training exercise in Belize according to the report.

Brody was now a Major in the SBS, but not a happy one. That night would never leave him; in his mind, he would always be a child killer.

# Chapter Three

*Pemba Island, Present Day*

The first sensation was a dull ache. It gradually increased, then the pain hit at the front of his head and worked its way around to the back until it was a non-descript pain covering his entire skull. The sun was streaming through the window. It must have been past 07:00. His mouth was like sandpaper, his tongue felt as though it had swollen to twice the size. He knew this feeling, the guilt and the shame of letting himself down, falling off the wagon. Brody thought he was safe on a Muslim island, but it always managed to find him, or rather he found it.

Struggling to get out of the bed, he staggered to the small kitchen where there was some bottled water. He sank into the chair and took a long pull on the bottle. It did not help much. It would take hours to shake this. After an age and a long, tepid shower in the small cubicle behind his bedroom, he was starting to feel human again.

Wandering out onto the beach, Brody spotted Hassan about 100 feet away in the shallows, throwing a net to pick the small fry living in the lagoon. The net was circular with weights draped around the bottom edge. Hassan was expert at throwing the net over a shoal of fish then pulling the top to catch the fish in the fine gill net.

Hassan saw him, then took one final swing of the net before collecting his wicker basket and heading over.

"Hujambo Bwana, Habari a Leo."

Brody was catching on. He answered, "Sijambo, Mzuri, Asante."

This was Swahili for, Hello, any news today? And, I am fine, it's nice and thank you. Brody was starting to enjoy this new, lovely, melodic language.

Hassan asked after his health, but Brody shook off the question, and grumbled," I'm fine, I was just tired."

They headed over to the jetty, along the path and through the village. It was a lovely day full of promise for anexcellent dive. The weather was hot, the sea was calm, and the sky was clear. Brody could see the small, wooden dhow, rocking gently at the side of the jetty. Everything was packed as agreed, ready for the dive. If only Brody had got up on time. His cheeks reddened, the thought of Hassan arriving at the jetty at 05:00, then having to wait until past 11. This was not good and would have to be made up for. In the Marines and the Special Boat Service, he had never been late, not for any reason on earth.

Brody's dream from the night before bothered him. Whenever it came to haunt his sleep, he could never forget those lost boys in Somalia: the cold, dead eyes, their bodies being ripped apart by his bullets. That had finished him for the service. He had become a Major so was not sent on missions anymore; just a desk jockey doing paperwork and training. It was not what he had signed up for and he soon became bored with the life.

That was the beginning of the end. When the tour was up, he decided to hang up his spurs and move on. He was here now looking for a new life purpose and to relax. He had no ties back home: no girl, no house or mortgage. Just him. He had decided to explore his beloved Africa to see if it offered him more, something to live for.

They reached the jetty and were getting ready to cast off. The small outboard had once again managed to start and was currently belching blue smoke into the air. It was not happy. Alongside the quay was a much larger dhow about fifty feet long, built from stout wooden planks all nailed together with long, handmade, steel nails. The dark wood shone from the shark and linseed oil, applied to ensure the wood stayed waterproof. There was a large stern deck set high so the captain could see over the bow. She was a real ocean dhow. These boats had sailed this coast from further south than Mozambique all the way to the Horn of Africa and beyond. Brody had seen them in Oman, Dubai, and many other Arab states on his various trips to those dry, dusty countries.

Brody had spent days aboard such boats when deployed behind enemy lines to do some infiltration or seek and destroy missions. The dhow is a sturdy craft made from wood. Many still have no engine so are difficult to spot on the radar. They travel at about 6 to 8 knots and leave no wake, moving well in the open ocean and having a relatively shallow draft ideal for sneaking up rivers and inlets. These ancient craft always looked old and dirty, so little attention was ever paid to them.

The curious thing was the sailing method. They used a lateen sailing rig. The boom is at the top of the mast, not the bottom. It's like the old sailing ships where block and tackle are all you have to pull this enormous length of wood up some thirty feet into the air. The boom is seated at a forty-five-degree angle to the deck. With no mainstay, the mast is secured through the deck into the hull. These masts are tree trunks with a circumference of up to 36 inches. The main and only sail is attached to the boom hanging above the deck. The sailors wrap the sail tightly and tie it off with palm fronds. When the captain orders it to be released, the first mate pulls the main sheet from the bottom of the boom. This breaks the palm fronds, letting the sail fall free to catch the wind. Once he has pulled the rope, he must run to the stern and tie off the main sheet before the wind catches the sail, or he could be thrown overboard.

Wooden dhows have been traveling the coasts of East Africa for hundreds of years, running along the coast on the monsoons. When the northeasterly winds are blowing they all come up from Mozambique, heading towards the Horn of Africa or their port on the way. They stay at the port, selling their wares and buying stock for the return home. When the monsoon changes in April-May, their captains set sail again on the South Easterlies back towards Mozambique. The winds are called the Kaskazi, which are the north easterlies, and the Kusi, which are the south easterlies.

Once struck the lateen sail is hard to maneuver. Tacking and jibing is a tough and dangerous job. This fifty-footer would be difficult to operate at sea. The crew must be experienced sailors.

The inside of the dhow was dirty and unkempt as a Marine, Brody hated to see dirty, dangerous ships afloat. The captain was angry and unsmiling. His crew looked rough and tough; wearing an assortment of shorts and jeans; not one was wearing a shirt. The men were lounging on the deck, smoking and looking as if they owned the whole town. They were a dangerous-looking bunch. Brody changed his mind about saying hello, which was the custom between fellow mariners.

These guys were trouble. He could sense it with every move they made. The crew of the ship looked at Brody with long, challenging stares. Their long knives attached to handles worn from years of use, hung loosely from their belts. The gang idled like a pride of lions waiting to pounce, looking totally relaxed, but ever watchful, not missing a thing happening around them. This crew of action knew no fear. They lived in the ocean, where life was precarious at the best of times. Brody knew this type of mob. He had met them in Afghanistan and Iraq. Desperate men like this were dangerous, very dangerous.

# Chapter Four

With the outboard complaining bitterly the dhow slowly chugged across the shallow lagoon, towards the small inlet that led them to the open ocean. Brody was deep in thought. After a while, he asked Hassan about the boat. Hassan said nothing for a few moments, he was deep in thought too.

"What is that boat all about?" Brody asked.

"It's Captain Faraj and his crew. They are bad men," Hassan said after a few minutes.

"Why?" Brody asked.

"Those pirates are smugglers of bad things up and down the coast; they make us sailors have an awful name with the government and cause soldiers to come and chase us all around the islands," Was Hassan's reply.

Brody had heard about the soldiers coming from the mainland and harassing the fishermen, saying they smuggled guns, slaves, drugs, and other contraband along the coast.

"So why is Captain Faraj here in Pemba?" Brody asked.

"He comes for food and supplies. He cannot get them in Dar-es-Salaam as they will arrest him. So he stops on the small islands and makes us give him supplies and sometimes fuel."

"That captain is a terrible man, a pirate. We should stay away from the jetty until the captain leaves. They will only do awful things when they are here. Allah is not happy when he sees these people on our island."

Pemba Island is only about 40 miles from the coast of Tanzania across the Pemba Channel, which is a shallow, rough piece of water dividing the islands from the mainland. Dar-es-Salaam, the capital city of Tanzania, is the first and primary port. This is where the government was. Faraj could not go that way without being arrested. Out here on the islands, there was very little if any law. The islands were run by elders, clan heads, and chiefs. The system worked pretty well. Most things were taken care of.

Pemba, where Brody was currently staying, is one of the largest islands sitting just north of Zanzibar, the capital of the archipelago. The group of atolls then spread themselves along the coast, all the way down to Songa Songa and Jewe island, some 240 miles to the south.

Brody put Captain Faraj and his crew of pirates behind him and set up the dive equipment for his two planned dives for the day. He was using standard aluminium AL80's, rented from a shop on the mainland, for his stay here. These tanks carry about 77 cubic feet of gas at 3000psi. This was plenty of gas for him. With well over two thousand personal dives and many more for the service, he had learnt how to control his breathing. Diving on your own is always said to be dangerous, however for an experienced person not pushing any limits, it is OK. Today the dives would be in 70 feet of crystal clear water with no obstructions. Hell, the boat was visible from the bottom. He could even dump his gear and swim to the surface in an emergency ascent without a problem.

Brody had practiced emergency ascents in the service many times from well over 75 feet. The trick is to know that the gas you are breathing at depth is much denser due to the external underwater pressure. Your first stage delivers air that you can breathe at local pressure. It is thicker than the air at sea level. As you ascend, it will expand in your lungs. He had to remember to let it dribble out of his mouth on the ascent to stop the expanding air from bursting his lungs. And the most important rules of all: do not panic! And swim slowly to the surface. His training officers always said: slow and easy, take a breath and never move fast underwater unless it's the last resort.

After setting the gear and checking the standard Scuba Pro regulators (the first stage had two regulators and a pressure gauge) and attaching his Suunto dive computer to his BCD, (Buoyancy Control Device) jacket, he was ready.

Next, Brody strapped a large, hefty, razor-sharp diving knife on his lower leg and slipped the small get-out-of-trouble knife into the pocket of his BCD. He was set. He did a final check on all of his equipment, tripled checked the air was turned on. This is a fatal mistake so many divers make. In the excitement to get into the water and dive, they forget to turn the air on. A couple of breaths are in the tubes joining the equipment, but that runs out quickly and the on valve is behind the diver's head almost out of reach.

Brody finally fitted his split fins sitting on the side of the boat. He gave Hassan the OK sign with his thumb and first finger. Blew a few breaths through the mouth tube of the BCD to inflate it a little, then back rolled off the boat. Surfacing, he tapped his head to show everything was OK, then emptied the BCD, heading for the reef below. Descending into the depths was always the most enjoyable experience for him, the feeling of weightlessness of his body as he slowly sank towards the bottom.

Brody felt elated, moving leisurely through the ocean, letting himself drop for a few seconds. Then flipped his head down. After a couple of strong strokes with his split fins, he was heading towards the bottom. The top of the coral reef was covered in luminescent fish. The colors were amazing. Bright orange, blues, and indigos, all the colors of the rainbow and many more. Nature was displaying herself all around him, just going about its business, oblivious to the new arrival. Life and death in this underwater microcosm.

The soft corals were beautiful in their own right, massive fan corals gently moving in the light current, blue soldierfish darting around their bright green, leafy branches.

The anemones, with the clownfish racing in and out of the bushy, multi-coloured tentacles a safe haven from predators. The poison from the anemones did not affect the small orange fish with the black and white stripes that Disney has made so famous. As Brody swam over them, they scooted back inside their poisonous home, then peeped through the forest at the huge passerby.

The massive, hard domed brain corals, in vivid green, sky blue, and dark purple, sat on the sand; their surface looking like a brain, ridged and valleyed. As Brody looked closer, he could see the magnificent multi-coloured flatworms; delicate creatures about one-inch-long, with fan-like edges fluttering over the coral. They had the most stunning designs covering their translucent bodies, colors from bright orange through to midnight blue.

The whole reef was alive with color and movement; everywhere you looked there was something new to see.

He had scuba dived in the UK where you cannot see your hand in front of your face. This place was like a 3D cinema, all around you was life and color always moving.

Brody headed down to 60 feet where the corals were larger and more mature, immersing himself in the environment which took his breath away. A large brown-spotted potato grouper with its broad mouth and full lips was lounging on some corals. As Brody approached, it lumbered off at a sedate pace. It must have weighed 100 pounds.

The reef was packed with life, like a busy city street. Small shoals of fish swam in and out of the soft and hard corals, larger groups of silver and white coley coley hung in the water just off the edge of the reef. So much to see. He played for a while, with for an octopus hiding under a stone. It was wonderful. Everything was forgotten: the dreams of the night before and the horrible Captain Faraj; Brody was lost in this underwater world where everything was quiet and peaceful. The warm ocean surrounding him, he felt totally at home in this weightless, serene environment.

Brody had slowly crossed the reef keeping his eye on his computer, bottom time, and the boat above him.

He was enjoying watching a giant honeycomb moray having her teeth cleaned by some intrepid bright blue and green cleaner shrimps. The fragile creatures seemed to be climbing right down this high-end predator's throat. Suddenly a noise startled him!

As always, his training kicked in, *"Do not panic, take a second, check your computer and your pressure gauge see how much air was left, still plenty, so there is no personal danger."*

The noise came again, the revving of an engine. It suddenly struck him this is what he had told Hassan to do if he needed him back on the boat for any reason. Brody had instructed Hassan to rev the engine as hard as he could three times, then leave it for thirty seconds then another three times until he saw Brody returning.

Brody could see the boat above; the prop was not spinning, but the exhaust from the propeller was churning the water. He wondered what could have possibly happened, then started swimming up straight away.

He had been down 56 minutes. The last 20 had been in less than 30 feet, so a safety stop at the five-meter mark was not required. However, he slowly ascended, not rushing. Whatever it was had to wait, or he could be useless easily getting nitrogen poisoning, or the bends as it was more commonly known, from coming up too fast after such a long dive.

He used the slow ascent to get as close to the tiny dhow as possible surfacing right beside Hassan.

"Bwana! Bwana, we must go!" Hassan shouted.

Brody asked, "Why?"

"There is trouble on the jetty, come quickly!" Hassan shouted, as he pointed frantically back toward the quay.

Brody gave him his gear then threw himself up the side of the dhow, twisting at the last second, ending up sitting on the gunwale with his fins dangling over the side. Hassan was already pulling the anchor from the sea bed. The boat was moving in less than three minutes. Brody looked at Hassan and thought to himself, *"This was an obvious emergency, Hassan never moved this fast!"*

# Chapter Five

After Brody and Hassan had left the sleepy African village, all had been well. The villagers went about their business making mats and thatching old broken huts before the rains came, the daily activities carried on in small villages all over the world. The old women chewed tobacco while showing the youngsters how to mill grain with a long wooden pole and a hollowed-out tree trunk, pounding the ears of corn until they were fine powder.

The men of the village had woken when the moon was still bright in the sky. After preparing breakfast, and attending first prayer in the small, white-walled mosque, which was rumored to be five hundred years old, they had prepared themselves for the day. Then set sail towards the open ocean, heading into the shallow waters and strong currents of the Pemba Channel, where they would catch the predatory pelagic tuna fish, sailfish, and dorado (dolphin fish).

The men would stay out for the whole day under the scorching heat with the southerly Kusi blowing them across the ocean, coming home only as the sun started to disappear behind the continent of Africa in the west. Wives waited patiently on the beach for their husbands to return. Once the boats were moored and the catch landed they would take the fish, selling what they could in the market, setting some to dry, and cooking the remainder for supper.

The madrassa school on the island opened early at 06:30 sharp. The young pupils, dressed in white kanzus or black buibuis, raced to the gate, terrified of the fierce matron who always took up station at the entrance. She carried a wicked-looking cane, waiting for latecomers. It was always the boys who felt her wrath, too many things to do on the way to school. After a thorough beating, the youngsters would have to pick the rubbish at lunchtime. The sun was only just up so the rooms were cool, but the metal roof would become sweltering by noon, passing its heat to the room below, making it impossible to teach the sweating, fidgety children.

The lessons consisted mostly of the Koran. The word of Allah was the word of law on the island. This was sprinkled with some mathematics, mostly rudimentary, then English as this was the language of the world. The girls all wore the traditional buibuis, a black gown covering them from head to foot. The young ladies did not have to cover their faces as they were still underage, but would need to when they reached puberty or got married. The girls were all studious and loved to learn. Some would be chosen to leave the island and head to the government university in Dar-es-Salaam, which was the goal of each one. They could then become doctors, lawyers, or teachers and earn a healthy living to help their parents and younger siblings, enabling the cycle to continue for the next generation as it had for a millennium.

The boys were more relaxed towards the school, but they had the option of fishing. If a boy showed no aptitude for the educational route, he was taken before he was twelve years old to the boats and would learn to fish next to his father or grandfather. This was the way of the island.

The school broke for lunch at 11:00. All the children rushed home to help their mothers and fathers with the chores of the day. The pupils returned at 16:00 for the afternoon session. As the sun finally beat its retreat, disappearing into the boiling ocean, they would head for the mosque for evening prayer, the boys in one section and the girls in another.

During the day, the main street was silent, just an occasional dog wandering around the center, looking for some shade to rest until evening came or mother hen with her chicks following her, scratching in the dirt looking for any tasty morsels. The only sound was the call to prayer from the ancient mosque, which happened five times every day, starting at 04:00 in the morning.

There was a small market in a brick-built building just next to the mosque. The old ladies who ran the stores chatted and argued as they sat among the mix of stalls, selling spices, fruits, coconuts, charcoal, and some meat. It was a very relaxed affair, mostly chatting, drinking sweet tea, and chewing tobacco. The brown stains covering the floor of the market showed its age.

It was mid-morning. The glaring sun was scorching, burning the lane that ran along the center of the village. The road was dusty and uneven, full of potholes since the last rains. The heat at this time made everything hot to the touch, almost unbearable. A lone dog yapping and a few goats braying were all that could be heard. They seemed impervious to the heat. Everyone was looking forward to the mid-day siesta, some had already settled into a shady spot to let the afternoon pass by.

Captain Faraj's dhow was empty. The crew were nowhere to be seen, even the captain had left his shaded cabin. Captain Faraj was on a mission. He knew this coast very well, having plied it for the last twenty years. Buying and stealing what he could, then selling the contraband to the highest bidder. The pirates had just finished a smuggling trip sailing off the coast almost forty miles due west, right out into the open ocean. This was not so good for him. Most dhow captains hugged the coastline. He had a small hand-held GPS which one of his contacts had given him, so was confident when he left he would find the shore again.

At the forty-mile mark, the captain used the GPS to take him to the waiting offshore trawler. He had picked up his prized packages of the white powder the 'Muzungus' loved so much, returning it to a small beach near Kilwa. Here he had met a fat Arab with a long flowing gown and extraordinarily long fingernails. The crew of cutthroats had landed the packages on the beach, then collected a large bundle of dirty one hundred dollar bills.

As the two businessmen sat having coffee on the beach the Arab mentioned he had a new deal. The captain, always on the lookout for a nefarious project with a good profit, sat up straight and started listening.

The fat Arab explained, "You see, Captain, there are a group of very wealthy men in Dubai looking for some permanent company for their households. Now, these young ladies must be untouched by the evil of man, young and virgins. All have to be good Muslims who live for Allah. If you could find such young ladies that were not spoilt in any way, I have willing and ready buyers in Dubai. It would be worth more than the white powder."

Captain Faraj smiled at the proposition. "Let's say I know of a place where I can find such valuable commodities. What do I have to do when I get hold of them?"

"It is simple really. You put them in your boat and meet me it the markets in Puntland."

The captain thought over the arrangement for a few moments then agreed to meet the fat Arab at the Horn of Africa in one month's time.

He had then proceeded to Pemba as the farthest north of the islands and very close to Kenya. He could easily grab some girls and be across the border before anyone raised the alarm. Once in Kenya waters, he would be out of the Tanzanian jurisdiction and home free.

Now he was putting his plan into action. His crew had gradually slunk off the dhow as the morning had passed by. They had wandered around in the village pretending to be interested in the market and walking along the lane. By mid-morning, the whole team had all surreptitiously made their way to the school. There were two at the rear of the building, watching the back entrance. The others were going straight through the front door.

Captain Faraj led his men into the school, marching through the front door to the small classroom. The air was stuffy from the sweltering metal roofs. The kids were studying hard, trying to concentrate in the heat. As the captain walked to the front of the room, he swiftly drew his pistol. The class teacher looked up from the blackboard with surprise as Captain Faraj, and two burly crew members approached him. The kids stared in disbelief at this intrusion. The teacher made to say something to the captain, but was cut off.

"No talking, I want silence!" The captain said.

All the students complied as they were terrified.

The captain went on, "All you girls stand up and move to the wall. The boys and you," he pointed at the teacher, "stay where you are!"

The girls slowly rose, the boys sat motionlessly. The teacher stood, watching, petrified at what was happening, dread filling his soul.

The captain looked at the twelve girls lined up against the wall. He walked along the line. He only wanted six, but the best six.

He said, "Open your mouths!"

Faraj inspected their teeth, then looked at their eyes and hair. He sent four back to their seats. The older ones and the ones with brown or stained teeth. The captain had eight now.

The teacher was watching him and his men walking around. He knew there were probably more outside. Fatma, the female teacher, suddenly walked into his classroom. She had heard the noise from across the hall and wondered what was happening. The two pirates by the door grabbed her and threw her into the room. She crashed across the desks, landing in a heap on the floor. The teacher rushed to her aid. The first pirate thought it was an attack. In a second he slipped his knife from its scabbard on his belt, stabbing it into the teacher's stomach. The teacher stopped in mid-step, looking down as the pirate pulled the eight-inch blade out of his belly large, dark, red stain appeared on his beautifully embroidered gray and blue kanzu.

Fatma screamed as she saw the red patch appear on the teacher. The second pirate kicked her across the room and she landed in a whimpering pile in the corner. The teacher crumpled to the floor and lay in a pool of his own blood.

The kids started screaming and crying. They had never seen such a thing in their lives. Captain Faraj grabbed the first girl pulling her towards the door.

Holding his pistol to her face, he shouted, "If you are any trouble I will kill them all."

The girls followed out of the school, as the captain was leaving he said, "Burn the place, it will cause a diversion."

They set off at a trot back to the dhow, five of the pirates and Faraj herding the girls along. People had heard the screaming and came out of their houses to see what the commotion was about. The women started screaming and crying as they saw their girls being dragged along the street. One elderly man stepped in front of the captain, raising his stick. Faraj punched him in the face, sending him careering over backwards with a broken and shattered nose.

The fire set by the men now started to be seen, the flames licking the edges of the roof of the school. The tinder-dry beams of the roof crackled as the fire took hold. Some villagers ran towards the fire as the children came streaming out, shouting and crying, looking for their mothers and safety.

Captain Faraj was nearly at the dhow when a group of men came running at him from a small lane. They had been on the beach and heard the commotion. The men ran straight into Faraj and his gang. The first few blows were from the wooden staves the men carried, but then the pirates, who knew how to fight, not like the fishermen, who were peaceful people, came into their own. One of the fishermen went down with a howl as a knife sliced his hand open to the bone. Another fell to the blow of a Turk's head knot on the end of a thick piece of rope. His head was split open and bleeding. The men were fighting, but losing badly. This would only last a moment longer.

As the pirates broke free from the melee, the captain pulled his pistol from his pants, firing into the air. Everything went silent. He pointed his gun at the girl he was holding and shouted, "Any more and she is dead, then you will all die the same way!"

When the pirates reached the dhow, they realized they only had six girls. Two had escaped during the fight. No matter, that was all he had promised the fat Arab anyway. He leaped aboard. The pirates pushed the girls along the gangplank onto the vessel.

Captain Faraj shouted, "Burn the jetty. Use those fuel cans!"

Three pirates rushed off towards a large stack of petrol cans, a delivery from the mainland.

He then turned to the bosun and said, "Get us underway, immediately!"

The dhow slowly reversed into the channel. Captain Faraj still held the girl, pointing the pistol at her head until they were far enough from shore to be safe. The jetty was now burning fiercely. In the distance, flames from the school at the top of the small rise in the town licked the air. The captain smiled. The villagers would be too busy to do anything for a few hours. He threw the girl to his crew who were pushing the others into the lower storeroom.

In eight hours, the dhow would be in Kenyan waters. Then an easy, trouble-free trip to the Horn to meet his new business partner. They would not return to these islands for a few years. He knew the Tanzanian government would be hunting the gang. Lamu or Kismayo might be a good place to hold up until it all cooled down. The sale of these girls, added to the cash from the white powder, might even give the captain enough to go and see his cousin in Dubai for six months.

He was grinning as he left the burning jetty behind him and as the dhow motored across the lagoon.

# Chapter Six

Brody and Hassan were heading back to the jetty as fast as the little dhow could move, which was not fast at all. The engine was on full revs, complaining bitterly. They saw the huge dhow of Captain Faraj moving towards them, heading towards the open ocean. The vessel was going to use the same cut to the sea as they had used for the diving trip.

Hassan shouted and pointed at the ship, saying to Brody, "You see! I heard shots and screaming. There is a fire in the town. Now Captain Faraj is leaving. Something terrible has happened!"

They headed onwards towards the jetty, hoping they could help in some way.

"Look, Bwana, they have our girls on the deck!" Hassan shouted.

Brody didn't understand what he meant. He was watching the fire in the village. Hassan had been on boats in the ocean since he could walk. All the fishermen here had fantastic eyesight. It amazed Brody how these people could walk along a dark path at night and see everything. Likewise, in the ocean, they could spot a shoal of fish from over a mile away. Hassan was jumping up and down and waving at Brody to look at the dhow in the distance. He had seen them moving some girls along the deck of the dhow towards the stern cabin. When he pointed it out to Brody, he could see a group of people all dressed in buibuis, the black cover that the Islamic ladies have to wear covering them from head to foot, so no man can feel lustful when seeing them.

Brody could see them now being herded back into a cabin. Without thinking, he told Hassan to make a course which would cross about 100 feet in front of the pirate ship. Hassan did not understand, but complied. They moved across in front of the slow dhow, Hassan cutting in front of the boat about 50 feet ahead. As he did so, Brody dived into the water, fins in hand. The pirates on the dhow were more interested in their current haul, and what was going on at the jetty, so did not notice Hassan

Brody waited, treading water. As the dhow was passing him, he grabbed a dangling bow line that had not been stowed properly. He was dragged along at midships, struggling to the side of the boat. First his fins, then his diving mask went into the wash. Clinging to the rope, he slowly pulled himself up along the side of the ship to where there was an old steel ladder a few feet out of the water. His plan so far was to climb onto the ship and rescue the girls. Not very well thought out. He did not know the number of pirates, their weapons, anything really.

The wake was rushing along the side of the boat, smacking him against the rough timbers. The waves were pouring into his throat as he gulped for air, trying to keep his head above the surface. His muscles were straining and burning, crying out to let go. He knew reaching the ladder was imperative or he would get sucked under the keel and into the spinning propeller.

Slowly and painfully, he approached the ladder. As soon as it was within reach he made a grab for it with his left hand, snagging the bottom rung, and hauled himself up. Even though the dhow was only going about four knots, it still made his arms and shoulders strain to breaking point as he dragged his body above the passing wake. Brody crouched at the bottom of the short ladder with burning arms, lungs full of water, and nasty scratches down his legs from the rough planks of the dhow. He took a few minutes to gather his breath and formulate a plan.

He moved cautiously up the old rusty ladder until he reached the top rung, then peered over the gunwale. On the deck, the thugs were getting the boat ready for their journey. He slid aboard silently, creeping behind a pile of ropes and boxes on the starboard side of the vessel. He moved slowly and carefully, inching his way along the deck always staying hidden from view. His very basic plan was to catch them off guard, maybe get rid of a couple over the side quickly. Then he would try to take the helm, and spin the wheel sending the dhow into the mangroves, where it would run aground. That at least would stop the abduction.

He moved vigilantly towards the first pirate and stepped up behind him. The only option open to him with no weapon was a fast-lethal suffocation hold. This had to be done quickly before anyone else on the deck noticed. Brody wrapped one strong arm around the guy's neck and put his hand over the man's mouth at the same time. This was not as quick as he would have liked, but it did the trick. No one was really paying attention. The guy went down and Brody dragged him behind the boxes.

The next one did not go so well. The thug turned as Brody was inches away and screamed out loudly to his shipmates before Brody right hooked him into unconsciousness.

Then all hell broke loose. He was in the fight for his life. Three huge, burly, guys came at him with wide, toothy, grins. These guys had seen action, probably from the time they were kids. This was trouble. Brody kicked the closest one's knee which sent him down, but only for a second. The next guy had a long rope with a huge Turk's head knot at the end and was waiting for his chance to crush Brody's skull. The thug in the center lunged. Brody backed away and punched the pirate in the kidneys. This only made him angry.

The first one was up and charging. Brody moved to the side of the attack and pushed the guy into the gunwale. There was a loud, sickening crack as his head smashed against the solid mahogany hardwood. He was down, but trouble was brewing.

Brody had allowed himself to be distracted by the charge and had made a grave mistake. The guy with the knot at the end of the rope swung with deadly accuracy. As he was turning back towards his attackers, the knot hit Brody on the edge of his jaw. The world started spinning. He staggered. This was not working out well. He was about to have all hell kicked out of him.

The third guy who had been kidney punched was now on his feet and mad. Brody slammed him in the nose with a straight right as he was coming up from his dizziness. It was more reaction than planning. Just to give him a second to think about how to get out of this with his life. The thug reeled back out of the fight with a broken and bleeding nose.

The rope came around again. Brody realized he had made another mistake. He had been maneuvered onto the gunwale, with nowhere to go. The last thing he remembered was the Turk's head coming for his face. He tried to duck, but was too slow. The huge rope knot hit him square in the face just above his nose. The blood-splattered as he tumbled back over the side of the boat into the water.

The next thing he knew Hassan was grabbing him by the shoulders and hauling him toward the small dhow. The pirates were in the distance, maneuvering through the cut and into the open ocean. As he watched, the dhow picked up speed, heading due north.

Brody was dazed and just laid down in the bottom of the boat until they reached the jetty. What he had tried was stupid and reckless, but he could not stop himself. It had just been reaction and training overriding his good sense. Now he was injured and bleeding, what help could he possibly be?

Faraj's escape plan had gone without a hitch, the jetty was an inferno of crackling dry wood with occasional explosions from the fuel drums. Hassan landed his dhow on the beach, his father and mother came running down towards them. His mother was in hysterics crying and screaming, "My baby! My baby!" The father was shouting in Swahili for Allah to help them with their problem.

Brody staggered off the boat dazed from the blow. His head was still spinning, blood was pouring from a gash on his forehead, the last ten minutes was repeating over and over in his brain. Could he have done better, moved more quickly or had a better plan? As usual, he was taking the blame for these thugs of the ocean. He looked at Hassan's mum and dad and instantly felt like he had let them down in some way.

Then it dawned on him. Where was Hassan's little sister? She was only fourteen. He did not really know what she looked like as he had only seen her face at dinner or when she served him coffee. But he remembered her lovely almond eyes and the beautiful flawless skin of her face. She was always smiling and happy to help, always talking to him using her English. The students were taught basic English at the local school, but they never got the chance to practice. When he had arrived, she had asked him so many questions about

England and the English. Now she was gone, taken by these monsters to God knows where.

That really pissed Brody off. All those years in the army and special forces had drilled into him a unique set of skills that he knew he could use on this occasion. He was going after those girls and bringing them back or die trying.

# Chapter Seven

The sun was slowly making its way down towards the end of the lagoon. Palm trees were silhouetted against the blazing orange glow as it disappeared into the ocean. Hassan's mother and father sat on the beach. His mum was moaning softly, his father with his head in his hands was still sobbing. Brody felt for him. Letting his daughter be taken by such brutes must bite hard. Any parent would feel the pain and regrets at what he could have done. He knew Hassan and his dad were grieving and would wonder, "what if?" for the rest of their lives.

Brody was determined. He hated this situation. It was just plain evil. The village was a happy place where kids could grow up in a great environment. This atrocity could not be allowed to happen. The six young girls that had been abducted were between fourteen and sixteen years old. Still children. They all went to the local school and were grade 'A' students. The village would miss them terribly. The girls were clever and would probably be chosen by the government school system to leave the island and be trained in the Dar-es-Salaam University. The university was a prestigious establishment that taught island girls, allowing them to make a real income which each girl diligently sent home, to help the village. Africa is an unforgiving place; everyone has to pull together to make life worth living. Now, these young ladies had been torn from their families and would disappear forever. The local authorities were understaffed, with little or no equipment. To try to get them on the case would take days. The navy would not be able to go into Kenyan waters, the Kenyans were unlikely to be able to help as relations were cordial at best. The situation was dire.

Brody pulled Hassan aside, asking him, "Where are these pirates going with your girls?"

Hassan said, "I have no idea. I have never been involved with pirates. They just disappear and then reappear whenever it suits them."

Brody was pushing for answers. He felt impotent right now. There must be something he could do. The anger inside him was boiling over, he kept pushing Hassan for information on how to get back at these evil men.

Out of desperation, Hassan said, "We could ask my grandfather. He was a fisherman many years ago and traveled on the big dhows, fishing the coasts of Kenya and Somalia and even went as far as the Horn."

Hassan's mother appeared next to Brody. She gently pushed him back to sitting on the sand. Then carefully set about dealing with his wounds. She applied a special liniment to rub on his jaw. It burned like hell. It smelt bad too, but she assured him it would pull out the bruise and make it leave. Then she washed his cut forehead and bound it with a bandage. The bleeding had stopped, but the cut was deep and his head ached.

Brody felt better after having his head sorted out. Now, with the brown ointment covering his jaw, he walked off the beach, thinking how to get back at these pirates. Hassan came jogging down the path, slightly out of breath with sweat beading on his forehead. It was now pitch black. Brody never understood how he could see so well.

Hassan said, "I have found my grandfather on the other side of the island chatting with his friends. We could go and see him now."

Brody said, "Let's go! What are we waiting for?" They took off at a fast jog back the way Hassan had come. Brody was happy to be in motion, at least trying to do something to help.

When they arrived at the rundown shack on the beach, four men were sitting around a small table, playing checkers with bottle tops. The tabletop had been painted like a checkers board. There was money on the table, and a surreptitious bottle on the floor, which everyone took particular attention not to notice as Hassan arrived.

Brody could see that these men had known the ocean all of their lives. They were laughing and bantering amongst each other in a good-humoured way. It reminded Brody of his soldiering days when everyone knew everyone and would have private jokes that any outsider just could not understand. Their bodies were old and broken, but their eyes were bright and full of mischief. The old fishermen had lived their lives to the fullest, and now were content to sit and retell the stories of their youth and the adventures on the ocean.

One particular old fisherman with a bent back and rheumy eyes was talking. "Back in my day, we would never let this happen. We had some backbone back then. Nowadays these youngsters are full of wind like the ladies from the mainland."

Another ancient man stood up, trembling, holding his walking cane. "You are right, Mohammed. We would have stopped these brigands before they got near the beach," he shook his stick in the air, "I can tell you I have beaten bigger men than that young captain. He was always bad. I knew his father, a young thief. It runs in their blood, you know."

The first man was tiring and looking for his chair. "I know back then we took their hides off if they were thieves. That soon stopped them. Nowadays their mothers protect them and what do we get? Just trouble, I tell you." Finished, he sat down in his chair, panting.

Hassan waited until there was a break in this rhetoric to ask if anyone would know the likely route of the pirates.

The old fishermen all looked at him like he was a slow child, and said in unison, "The Horn, they will go straight to the Horn."

His Grandfather then chipped in, "And sell our lovely girls to the Arabs."

This they agreed on unanimously. It was obvious to them. They explained to Hassan and Brody that as this was the Kusi and the dhow was a fifty-footer with only a tiny engine, the captain was cheap. There had no choice, the only way was north. The wind would take them all the way to the Horn. Then the pirates could find ready buyers for their human cargo.

One of the old fishermen said, "The Arabs have been buying slaves for hundreds of years. Zanzibar used to have the biggest market in the Indian Ocean."

The old gay was getting his steam up now. And went on with his story, "It was the largest in the world. The Sultan of Zanzibar used to sell the slaves to all comers from America, Europe, and the Middle Eastern States. It was only when the Queen of England got angry and did not want them selling anymore that she sent a massive battleship to tell the Sultan to stop. The Sultan of Zanzibar would not listen to those 'Muzungus,' he refused and sent the captain back to his warship."

The fisherman laughed as he recounted the story, "The captain got so mad, he fired his guns at the Sultan's Palace in Zanzibar."

All old men were holding their stomachs now as they cried with laughter. They all spoke at once, "When the 'Muzungus' fired their cannons, the Sultan ran away like a chicken being chased. He pulled up the white flag after about five shots from the 'Muzungus.'"

"It was the shortest battle ever in the history of 'Muzungu' warfare. The Sultan acted like a spoilt girl and was sent back to the Middle East. The slave market was shut for good!"

However, that did not stop the pirates from going underground and stealing people, taking them all the way to the Horn of Africa, some fifteen hundred miles to the north where the slave markets still flourished to this day, as they had seen with their own girls being abducted.

Hassan's Grandfather was a skinny-legged old man, who had sat on a boat all of his life. He must have been sixty or maybe older, it was hard to tell. He had soft gray hair, hidden mostly under his multi-coloured turban, and was dressed in a white robe with shorts underneath. When he sat, he lifted the robe onto his lap to keep cool. He had rough, callused hands that had seen years of manual labor, with clear, bright shining eyes, he did not miss a thing. The old man banged his lovely, silver, topped walking stick on the ground to get everyone's attention.

He said, "Captain Faraj will cross over to Wasini on the southern tip of Kenya, then start heading north along the coast. He is sneaky, so will stay about eight to ten miles offshore, just over the horizon. He is cunning, and won't want any prying eyes interrupting his now very profitable journey."

Brody said, "Can anyone give me directions to follow?"

Hassan's Grandfather said, "Of course. It's easy to follow them, just like following a shoal of fish in the ocean, just watch the waves and the birds above."

Then he banged his stick again and said: "No this is my granddaughter, and many more granddaughters. We will find them together. I am not so old I cannot sail a rig and live on the sea!"

Hassan said, "No, Mzee, you are an old man and should not travel in this way, your health will suffer."

Hassan yelped as the walking stick caught him across his shins, sending him hopping out of the room. This old guy was tough. In his prime, he would have been a formidable character.

The group agreed to let the Mzee have one of the family dhows, a much larger dhow than Hassan's. The boat had been built in Lamu, so could go faster and was designed with the rougher seas in mind. They agreed to meet at dawn at the jetty where the dhow would be ready, and they could set off.

The mzee said, "It will take at least seven days, sailing day and night. We will need one more good seaman on the boat."

Hassan agreed and went off to look for his friend Gumbao, an old sea dog that lived on the island.

Brody spent the rest of the night preparing. Hassan's mother cooked loads of 'mahamry,' a deep-fried cake, and 'biryani,' a local delicacy of rice, goat meat, and vegetables. Enough supplies to sustain them for a couple of days at least. Brody filled the dive tanks, collected his dive gear, and prepared his equipment, wishing silently he had a gun of some kind. But he knew there were none on the island. After a short nap, Hassan shook him awake. It was still pitch dark. Laconic waves lapped against the burnt-out jetty, blown in from the south-east, as the group collected on the sandy beach.

Hassan's grandfather with his stick, a hat, and a pair of very-cool wraparound blackout sunglasses was standing on the beach like he owned it. Hassan's father and mother were there also as they waited for the dhow to come around from further along the lagoon. Brody had his tanks, speargun, both dive knives, and anything else he could think of. Hassan spotted the dhow rounding a small headland about 300 feet away.

Mzee said, "Gumbao looks in good health." Brody was shocked. He could hardly make out the boat it was so dark.

Gumbao approached carefully. The dhow had a small 25hp engine on the back for maneuvering. As he approached the beach, Hassan grabbed the bow, stopping the boat from digging into the sand. The new crew loaded the equipment and food silently and were bidding their farewells when they heard a shout from the end of the beach. A middle-aged guy was running towards them. Hassan jumped out of the dhow to meet him. The man was tall and gaunt, with a wispy moustache and bright red beard, which had been coated with 'Henna,' traditional leaves plucked from plants found on the island then ground into a paste and mixed with water to color the beards of the elders. He had the usual Muslim garb (dressed all in white, with a black waistcoat) with a small flat turban on his head. The man seemed nervous as he approached, he had a box in his hand, and insisted on speaking to Brody. Brody jumped out of the boat and approached him, the man was the village Head Elder called Jamal.

Jamal whispered to Brody, "I am so shocked about this attack. It is most terrible. Our poor girls and their families, this is truly awful. I will pray to Allah now for a safe return of our precious girls from the hands of these pirates."

Jamal paused before going on, "I would go with you, but I am afraid I have to stay to see to the rebuilding of the jetty and making sure this will not happen again."

Jamal handed Brody the box, which was surprisingly weighty. Brody looked questioningly at the tall, gaunt man.

Jamal said, "As the Head Elder of this island, I have the honor of holding the government issue firearm. It has never been used. I have kept it in the drawer of my desk for these last few years. I hope it works. You must take it, as this is official business of the island. I am deputizing you to help us find our girls. All you 'Muzungus' know how guns work and are experts in firing them."

Brody thanked the man and accepted the gift, hoping it was not just some rusty piece of junk. The Head Elder then said goodbye and headed for the mosque to start the first prayers. The crew left immediately, heading for the open sea.

Back on-board, Brody carefully opened the box. He was not expecting much. How long the gun had been in the Head Elders office in the drawer? Just forgotten. The box was heavy mahogany which had been made with care, the lid was hinged and greased. Brody gingerly lifted the lid to find an oilcloth inside. He lifted the heavy gun out, immediately knowing he was holding a Glock, probably a 17 from the feel of it. These were very handy weapons used throughout the world by police officers. The gun had first been introduced in the early eighties to the Austrian military and from there it had blossomed into one of the most used handguns in the world. The weapon had a magazine that took ten rounds plus one in the chamber. The gun was ideal for the military and the police as it could be easily disassembled, cleaned, and reassembled without specialized tools.

As he opened the oilcloth, his thoughts were confirmed. This was a Glock 17 first generation, the oldest. The weapons had probably been donated to Tanzania from Austria when they upgraded their weaponry.

The gun was old but had not seen much action. It was oiled and clean. Brody dismantled it expertly: he could see it was in excellent condition. After a quick clean, and testing of the firing mechanism, it looked good. The box also contained an envelope with twenty rounds of standard N.A.T.O 9mm ammunition. This all looked good too. There was a note in the box, it said '**Only to be used if The Island is Under Threat From An Invading Party.**' The official note was stamped by the OCPD of Dar-es-Salaam.

Brody felt much better: he now had a gun, a spear gun, and a knife. That would even the odds a little. He would not get beaten this time.

The tip of the blazing orb was just starting to make itself visible on the horizon. There were golden streaks of light like a halo racing up into the clouds above. The boat was motoring along slowly on a flat ocean; it was like a millpond at this time of day as the sun started to rise. Brody shivered. The breeze was cold on the sea before the sun crawled above the horizon, then it would beat down on them relentlessly all day. Before leaving the island, he had not been able to see the dhow as it was dark, but now with the sun rising, it was a good time to inspect this boat, and their new friend Gumbao.

The dhow was very different from Hassan's. The vessel was not so much a vessel for hauling large loads. It had long sleek lines. The bow was very pointed and high. With a beam of about 16 feet at midships, but both bow and stern were more tapered. The dhow was about 36 feet long with an open deck forwards and a small cabin at the rear, with the wheel in front of the cabin. The cramped cabin was only good for sleeping in. The forward deck was where the crew would spend the whole time. The mast was set slightly forward of amidships. It had a definite angle on it, pointing towards the bow. Mzee said, this was to give greater speed through the water.

They had chosen this dhow because it was built for speed. A fishing boat that would go out of port and stay fishing for about three days before returning. Mzee told them, the dhow was designed to outrace the wind and cut the waves like a knife.

Brody was not much of a sailor. He had been on boats all of his career in the forces, but they had engines and propellers. All this one had was a small outboard pushing them at about 6 knots.

After checking out the new boat, Brody shifted his attention to their new shipmate. Gumbao was about five feet, six inches tall, dressed in blue shorts and a scruffy torn T-Shirt. He had a cap on his head stating he was the captain in bold white letters. When he smiled, he had two front teeth missing on his upper and lower jaw, with short stubbly white hair and a wispy beard. His fingers were bent the way only a man who has lived with his hands in the ocean dragging nets and pulling on ropes can look. He would have made any manicurist cry; his fingers had seen a lot of hard work. He sat on the deck, with his broad, flat foot on the wheel keeping them on course, continually looking at the ocean around him. This guy was a professional seaman; you could tell he was relaxed, but knew good old Mother Nature could change her mood in a split of a second.

They cruised along, crossing the twenty-five miles of the open ocean towards Wasini island, the end of Tanzania and the beginning of Kenya. Getting the dhow and crew ready had cost twenty-four hours, which was a long time, giving Faraj and his crew time to get at least 80 miles ahead of them.

The Mzee said "We must catch them before Somalia. Once those villains cross the border, it will be almost impossible to catch them: the Somalis are 'Macorras.'"

"Bad people," Hassan explained.

The waves started to get the tops gently knocked off about two hours after sunrise. The old Mzee had taken over the position of navigator and made a course heading northeast along the coast. As soon as the wind hit them,

Gumbao gave Brody the wheel, then ran to the bow with Hassan. They expertly pulled the boom to the top of the mast. Hassan pulled the end of the boom down to him with the sheet for the sail. The sail had been rolled tight against the boom, and tied off with thin coconut fronds. While Gumbao rushed back to Brody to take the wheel, Hassan pulled the sheet. The coconut fronds broke, letting the sail fill with the southeasterly.

As the sail filled, Hassan ran back with the sheet in his hand, looping it around a wooden pillar on the starboard side. The triangular sail billowed out on the port side. Hassan started tightening the sheet under Gumbao's instructions. Together they worked to get the sail in exactly the correct position to make a dead run along the east African coast.

Once the wind filled the sail, Brody was amazed at how fast the small dhow started cutting through the swell. The bow lifted then dipped as they crossed each long wave. Their headway was surprising. This boat was built for speed! The sleek, wooden craft must have been doing ten knots now and holding. The wind gradually increased through the morning as they continued along the coast, passing Mombasa port at around 14:00 and continuing on towards Malindi, some thirty miles further along the coast.

As the sun started to dip below the mainland on the second day, they were nearing Formosa Bay, a large gash in the coastline marking the natural boundary between Kenya and Lamu. The bay meant the end of civilization for the next two hundred miles. The small outpost of Lamu being the only safe haven. Long sandy beaches marked the edge of a coast that was as it had been for hundreds, if not thousands of years. Wild animals roamed the bush and even on the beach.

Mzee said, "We will stop at Ziwayu on the northern side of Formosa Bay. There we will ask the shark fishermen what they have seen."

The shark fishermen who lived on the small rocky island knew who passed day or night. Most boats would stop there to pick up some provisions from the little shop that existed on this tiny outcrop.

The huge moon shone down on them as they crossed the bay. In the evenings the wind calmed for a couple of hours, so they cruised at 4 knots. The outboard was running to help them keep moving. Their supplies were running low and their stomachs were starting to grumble. Brody hoped this island would provide some sustenance.

As the sun came up in the east, Gumbao spotted the island just to the west of them. Mzee had been working on dead reckoning, no GPS or even a sextant to spot where they were. Altering course, they came into the island from the southwest on the deep-water approach. The island was just a coral rock sticking out of the ocean about two miles offshore. On the atoll were six little-thatched huts. A small swirl of smoke was coming from the center of the island. Apart from that, it looked empty.

The sea birds squawking and arguing over scraps on the beach were the only noises breaking through the silence.

Moored on the beach were about a dozen different shaped vessels all laying in the shallows on the lee side of the coral rock. As they approached, Brody felt his eyes start to water, then he began sneezing. A disgusting smell was permeating the air. The others did not seem to notice. It smelled like something had died there not so long ago and was rotting on the rocks under the boiling hot sun.

Hassan said, "This is where you get the best-dried shark meat. Excellent for cooking."

On the ocean side of the island, there was a massive drop off down to three hundred meters almost vertically into the ocean. The North Kenya Banks were thirty miles further offshore. A world-renowned fishing area, Hemingway had fished those grounds for marlins and sailfish in the 1940s.

Gumbao expertly edged the dhow up to the beach, being careful to keep the boat afloat. Mzee wanted to be able to leave at a moments notice, not having to wait for the tide. The small, eclectic crew's feet burnt as they walked across the golden sand, stepping into the small pools spotted across the beach for relief. There were hundreds of gulls sitting on the sand, waiting for the day to start. When the wind came up, they would all head out to sea for a day's fishing.

The group found themselves at the bottom of a small wooden ladder which led up to the island. As they climbed up, a head appeared over the top and greeted 'Mzee,' Hassan's Grandfather. Brody realized that any older man was called 'Mzee.' It was a term of respect. These guys both looked to be well into their sixties, but they seemed to remember each other. 'Mzee' was soon sat chatting animatedly to his long-lost buddy. He explained to them the piracy attack and the abduction of the girls from the island. The shark fishermen were shocked at such an atrocity. The island shark fishermen could not believe that Swahilis would do this to each other. 'Mzee' then described the dhow and the crew in detail as if he knew them. The men on the island had seen this dhow. The captain had come over to the island just last night to buy 'Papa,' shark meat and 'Unga,' a ground maize meal to make ugali, the staple diet of the East African.

This was good news. They were on kidnappers tail and heading in the right direction. Brody mentioned this to the Mzee, but he just shook his head and said, "Of course, it is the only way!"

Captain Faraj's dhow had stayed off the island, sending in a small cutter they kept on deck, so the fishermen had, had no idea there were abducted girls on the boat. They had provided the captain with what he had asked for. When he was leaving, the captain had said, *I am probably pulling into Kiwayu just before the Somalian border. There are some safe moorings in a hidden, sheltered cove with deep water so easy to stay out of sight for a couple of days.*

The old fisherman explained that Captain Faraj could then restock with food and supplies as Somalia was rubbish and expensive. It was a barren place with nothing to buy and full of militia who just stole everything. The Somalian coastline is long and very rough with few places to stop and shelter. With long rock-strewn beaches open to the ocean and few offshore reefs to protect the lagoons. This stretch of coast was dangerous even to pirates. It was about one thousand miles long. Traveling at eight knots it would take them about a week to get to the Horn.

Brody and his crew soon headed off. They needed to reduce the distance quickly before the pirates escaped into Somalian territory. As soon as they were underway, Hassan, who had bought a good-sized dorado from the fishermen, started preparing the meal. He lit the 20-litre jerry can which was their stove, putting a pot of water on the fire for the 'Ugali,' A local meal made by boiling the water, then slowly mixing the maize meal in with a stick until it becomes like porridge. He put the pan as close to the heat as possible, stirring it quickly until it became a solid mass, then tipped it out on the plate. Everyone took handfuls, squashing it in their hands and eating it with the boiled fish. The fish was soup, just chopped up and dropped into a bucket of boiling seawater, head and all, with a small chunk of shark meat, which made the soup stew incredibly salty and tasteful. Once Brody got used to the smell!

They relaxed for the rest of the morning, traveling with the shore to the west, just in sight on the horizon, some eight miles away. The 'Mzee' knew where this bay was and was thinking of the best approach. Brody had been thinking of a plan but really could not do much until he could see the situation. They sailed on, passing Lamu at noon, gliding across the quiet ocean as the day wore on. Occasionally, a flying fish would leap out of the water ahead of them, zooming over the flat calm ocean, then diving back into the water once the danger from below had disappeared.

Hassan decided he had to stop the boredom. He said, "Mr Brody, you know that Lamu has been a trading port for us Swahilis for many years. Vasco De Gamma from Portugal came here in the 1400s. There is even a fort built in Mombasa where he lived. Back then we Swahili were good at business and had loads to sell, so Lamu was very busy. My father says his ancestors sold spices, ivory, gold and many other things from the interior of Africa. Ah, but now it is just a sleepy village, full of lazy people. About fifty years ago, loads of 'Mzungus' came and smoked bangi. It spoilt the place.

Brody replied, "I visited it a few times when I was in the army. A great place for a week. Lovely beaches and plenty of booze, but if you stay too long it is easy to get lost in the place. So relaxing and just nothing to do all day!"

"That's true, Mr Brody, many people come and never leave. There are no cars there, everyone has to move around by donkey, the streets are just too narrow. That and the houses all built up one on top of the next. But life is cheap and there is always loads of fresh fish to eat."

The thirty-foot boat easily cut through the swells. It was made for this type of journey, a long, thin dart. Gumbao sat silently in the stern, his foot moving the tiller a little to port or starboard to keep the sails full. The dhow was doing a good eight knots, but they still had quite a way to go before reaching the small, hidden cove. If their journey had not been a desperate race to save the young girls, it would have been idyllic to sit on the deck, watching the East African coast go slowly by. The beach was beautiful with rugged, steep dunes rising up some sixty feet, the flat, unblemished sand running for miles, not a house, or a person in sight. This really was a paradise lost. The small dhow passed the large entrance to Lamu harbor and then on past Pate Island heading north towards Somalia.

As Pate Island receded into the distance, Hassan broke the silence once again. "Mr Brody, this is a wild area. There are no police or soldiers here, just wild animals. The islands are spread out all the way up to Kismayo, the first port of Somalia. Inland, there are thousands of waterways dividing up the tiny islands and coves, you could get lost in there forever. Those guys of Lamu say you can sail a boat all the way to Somalia in the secret passageways."

Brody nodded and thought to himself, "Exactly what I am looking for. No witnesses." He was still brooding over the beating he had received on the dhow a few days earlier. His jaw still ached, and the cut on his head would take weeks to heal. He was angry and wanted revenge. He also wanted to free these young girls with so much to live for. He could not bear the thought of them turning into the poor children he had shot all those years ago in Somalia. For all he knew, those poor boys he had met in the village, holding their AK's and killing his friend, had started life out in a small village like Hassan, before they had been abducted and forced to train as young                    child                    soldiers.

# Chapter Eight

The moon was high, shining from a cloudless night. The stars had come out, filling the sky to capacity. Brody felt he could almost reach out and touch the Milky Way it seemed so close. But all around them was pitch black. The dhow motored through the inky waters, about five hundred feet off the jagged reef. Hassan, Mzee, and Gumbao silently watched the shore. All Brody could see was a vague surf line in the distance, and he could hear the waves breaking on the exposed reef. He looked east out over the glistening, flat ocean: the moon was rising, giving an ethereal glow to the water.

They had been traveling for an hour in silence. Brody knew they must be getting close to the inlet by now. The tension on the small craft could be cut with a knife. Mzee was staring towards the breakers. Brody could hear them, but only see a faint white line in the distance. The waves hitting the reef were thundering as they rolled up and over the top of the rocks. With no points of reference, the darkness was deceiving. It was impossible to gauge distance. Brody had no idea how far from the shore or the reef they actually were.

Gumbao motioned to Mzee to look at the beach. Brody wondered what they could possibly be looking at, it all looked the same to him. Mzee and Hassan stood and moved to the bow. Once the two lookouts had settled they started giving directions in Swahili to Gumbao. He listened intently and did exactly as he was told.

Hassan said, "Kushoto, Kushoto!" Left, left.

Then Mzee would pipe in with "Pole, Pole, Enda Moja Kwa Moja!". Slowly, slowly go straight on!

Brody was lost. He couldn't see anything in this light. He was amazed at how sure they were, working in unison, the total trust of people together on the ocean, knowing implicitly each is responsible for the life of the other.

Brody felt the stern of the craft get lifted by a wave. His stomach shot up into his mouth. Gumbao had turned west, heading straight for the reef line. It was impossible to see the surf. Waves could be clearly heard breaking on the shore ahead of them. The dhow was lifted and pushed forward. The second wave was nearer breaking. Brody saw it passing the gunwales of the boat. It must have been 4 feet high. This was madness. They would surely get smashed against the rocks. The next wave lifted the stern of the boat, this time much higher, pushing them much quicker towards the now crashing surf. As the wave passed under the craft, the stern fell into the trough before the next one rolled through. Brody was sure now they would be hit by a wave and smashed into the rocks.

Gumbao was struggling with the wheel to keep the craft from swerving broadside to the swell and flipping the boat. This had all happened in the split of a second.

Brody could not even see the waves in front of them. It was eerie handing his safety over to these guys. The next wave picked the stern. The deck was at almost 35 degrees. The craft was surfing down a wall of water. Brody could see the surf on either side of them beginning to break. This was going to be a disaster, if the wave broke it would push the small boat to the side, and they would get flipped in an instant. Their wave held though, as the ones on either side broke over the rocks. The dhow shot across the top of the reef, through a small opening that was almost invisible. The wave carried them right through the narrow gap at about 12 knots until it dissipated in a small lagoon. Brody looked back and could see the surf breaking on either side of the entrance. He had not noticed, but his knuckles were white as they gripped the gunwale of the small craft.

The boat and crew were through into the quiet lagoon. Hassan and Mzee were still out in front looking for a suitable place to tie up and get ready. No one seemed that bothered about the near-death experience. He was amazed at their skill. In his days in the army, he had used satellite imagery, GPS, electronic charts, and NVGs. These two guys, with an old man, had managed to navigate a small gap in the reef in total darkness, without any of the equipment he would have needed. It was unbelievable.

They found themselves in a small inlet. The lagoon had been formed over the millennia and was about six feet deep of calm water.

Mzee said, "The dhow is moored about 3 miles over the hill in front. If we move now, we can be there while it is still dark to get a lie of the land."

The mangrove swamp they had to get through was old. The roots were deep, in the soft, thick soil. It was like spaghetti on a plate, but each gnarled root was hard as stone. Climbing through these old twisted branches left his ankles sore and bruised. They finally reached the glittering white sand of the small beach below the cliff.

A steep limestone wall faced them. It glowed in the moonlight. Old worn goat tracks crisscrossed it at intervals all the way to the summit, some sixty feet above. They slowly made their way along the rough, narrow paths. When one ended, they would jump up to the next and continue. The soft, pale light of the moon reflected off the yellow stone, giving enough light to find the handholds in the cliff face. The climb was arduous. After sitting still for so many days, their limbs were stiff.

Once they reached the top, Faraj's dhow was clearly visible in the lagoon below. It was moored at the southern end of the creek in what Mzee said was the deepest part. The dhow was anchored with the bow pointing north towards the ocean end of the inlet. The water had a slight chop to it as the waves were rolling in through the narrow cut in the reef. The inlet was about two hundred feet across east to west, the shape of a beer bottle from north to south. With the cut, or entrance, about a quarter of the way along the neck of the bottle on the eastern side.

Now, what to do? Brody signaled to the other three. Everyone moved back off the brow of the hill. Brody needed information to put a plan together. He sent Hassan and Gumbao back to their boat for his diving equipment. He would approach the dhow, find out as much as possible, then formulate a plan to free these young girls.

Once Hassan and Gumbao had returned, Brody decided to approach the dhow from the bow. The water was choppy from the inlet and would hide the bubbles from his scuba gear. If he approached at a depth of 30 feet, he would be able to reach the bow of the vessel without being seen. Then, using his skills from his Special Boat Service training, he would do a full recce of the ship, its occupants, and captives.

Brody carefully slipped into the water at the edge of the mangroves lining the bay, disappearing from sight almost immediately. He moved along the bottom, holding himself just off the mud to ensure he was completely submerged and did not create a disturbance on the surface. He shone the underwater torch on the depth gauge. It started to faintly glow. The screen would luminesce for about twenty minutes. When the gauge read thirty feet, he slowly lifted himself off the bottom. Using his BCD, Buoyancy Control Device, he maintained neutral buoyancy. He moved through the darkness as silently as he could. Taking long slow breaths on his regulator to stop the larger bubbles forming, which would expose his position to any keen-eyed watchmen standing on the bow of Faraj's boat.

Underwater navigation is a nightmare. There are no landmarks to use. This, combined with currents and not know your speed, make it almost impossible to maintain a course. However, after years of training, Brody had a second sense which allowed him to gauge speed and distance underwater, even at night. He used his left arm to point in the direction, then bent his right arm and grasped his left with his right hand. Now the compass was right in front of his mask. The glowing gauge pointed almost south-west. The bearing he had taken before submerging was 242 degrees to the bow of the boat. Brody used measured kicks to get him to where he thought he was about twenty feet from the dhow. He slowly ascended until he could see the moonlight shining above, then waited. His training had taught him if anyone had seen his bubbles they would probably raise the alarm now. With two feet left, he held his breath, then slowly rose until his head broke the surface just to eye level. The dhow was just in front of him. All was quiet.

He slowly swam with just his eyes out of the water towards the bow of the dhow. This was the critical time. If he was spotted now, the plan was dead, and the whole mission would go down the drain. All would be lost.

Brody swam along the port side of the boat until he reached the stern. The huge wooden rudder was sitting under the hull in the shadows. Slipping out of his BCD, he clipped it to a bolt just below the waterline. With only his mask, snorkel, and fins he could move more quickly around the large dhow. He slowly made his way back along the starboard side of the boat. His SBS training had taught him how to go through the water without making a sound. On the journey, he periodically stopped and listened for any noise or chatter from the deck. It was silent. According to his Rolex Submariner, the time was nearing 04:00 hours. The best time to approach as even the watchmen were feeling drowsy.

Brody swam to the anchor line. It was a three-twist hawser laid rope, encrusted with salty grime, two inches thick, and very old. The grimy rope had seen better days and was suffering from the thousands of times it had been run in and out over the many years of service. He slowly and carefully climbed the rope until he could get a foothold on the running strip. Then he let his feet dangle out of the water and pulled himself up with his arms to peer over the gunwale. The deck was bathed in the moon's glow. It was relatively easy to see the layout. The forward section had several large wooden crates, and some ropes loosely coiled on the floor. There were two sleeping bodies laid out on rough sleeping mats behind two more crates further along the deck. Brody could see the aft cabin where the girls had been herded. Above, and taking up the whole rear of the dhow, was a long covered section. This is where the captain slept. It also provided good cover from the elements for the guards to keep watch over the complete length of the vessel.

Brody could see one of the guards was nodding his head trying to stay awake. The other was slumped in a straight back chair, gently snoring. He was cautious, remembering what these guys could do. He had taken them on before unprepared. Just three had dealt him some severe blows, knocking him off the boat altogether. The cut on his head was still painful to touch. There must be another couple of guys sleeping somewhere else. At the jetty in Pemba, there had been six.

He slowly lowered himself back down the rope into the lagoon. A plan was formulating: with some help and more weaponry he could at least hold his own. Brody swam silently back to his scuba gear, then, after taking a reciprocal bearing, headed back to the mangroves.

# Chapter Nine

Brody had been trained during his years in the forces to plan attacks and extractions. This had the potential to be both. During his many years working all over the world, two main principles had shone through: the first was called KISS, which in army speak meant, Keep It Simple Stupid, meaning the best plan was always the simplest. Complications meant mistakes. The second principle was: as soon as the first shot was fired all plans went to hell.

Keeping this in mind and then building in the factor that he had a young boy, an old man, and a dhow captain as his extraction force, the plan was formulated. After some serious considerations, he decided to send Mzee and Hassan in the small dhow to approach the inlet from the open ocean to where Captain Faraj was moored. There was a headland so they could come in slow and easy, then hold up two or three hundred feet from the larger dhow. Hassan and Mzee would be on the lee side of the island, out of the moonlight's range, waiting in the shadows until they got a signal from Brody to approach.

Brody and Gumbao would go back and board the dhow. Armed with the pistol and the speargun. The pirates looked very relaxed in their secret haven. Even the guards seemed to be dozing. Brody felt confident he and Gumbao could board the ship and take them by surprise, hopefully before they could get their guns out.

When it was over and the crew had been subdued, they would free the girls, signal to Mzee to come alongside and collect them all, then make good their getaway. It was a very simplistic plan. Brody didn't have half a dozen operators with him and all the hi-tech equipment, so there was a lot of winging it, hoping and praying. If only Dave and the crew were here to watch his back, this would be a walk in the park.

Brody put these negative thoughts out of his head when he was explaining to the team what their roles were. Hassan objected as Brody knew he would. The boy wanted to be in the fight. It was his sister after all. But Gumbao was older. Brody could see just by the way he held himself he was not shy in a brawl, with hands like shovels, and muscles that had been trained every day of his life by the ocean, the toughest gym in the world. Brody was sure he could take a beating and get up for work the next day. If you lived in the ocean, it changed you. Gumbao had fought the waves for years and was still here to tell the tales. Living the life Gumbao had, he was very lucky and skilled to have made it this far. Brody knew men. He had trusted soldiers many times with his own life. Watching Gumbao's quick wits and fast decision-making skills put him ahead of the rest, a good risk in a fight.

When the plan was agreed upon Brody gave Gumbao the spear gun and showed him the basics. There would only be one shot from that, it had to count. Then Brody checked the Glock, making sure it had a full magazine and one in the chamber. The team were ready for the assault, no comms, no backup, and no help if it all went wrong.

"Well, here goes nothing," Brody muttered under his breath.

The idea was for Gumbao to approach from the starboard side and find the rusty old ladder Brody had used when he boarded the boat in Pemba. Gumbao would climb the ladder and wait just below the gunwale until he could see Brody boarding.

Brody would climb the anchor rope again. They would take out the two guys that were sleeping on the mats first, then move onto the guards, and hopefully, have the captain tied up inside of 8 minutes.

Brody climbed the slippery old rope, being as quiet as possible. He reached the gunwale and nimbly jumped, landing on the forward deck, his bare feet making no sound. Once there, he quickly checked the immediate surroundings. All was as before. He slunk across the deck then ducked down into cover. In the shadows of the packing crate, he had time to analyse and situation and get ready. He retrieved the Glock from the waterproof pouch and checked it. He held the top slide, slowly pulling it back to make sure a round was in the chamber. Finally, he made sure his dive knife was unclipped and ready for fast release.

He silently moved forward. Gumbao's head and eyes were in view on the starboard side. He signaled with his hand towards the two sleeping figures. Gumbao came over the gunwale like a cat stalking a prey and met Brody next to the large crates. The first two pirates were asleep behind them, thankfully out of sight of the main cabin.

Before the first sleeper knew it, Brody held him in a stranglehold. The thug tried to cry out, but Brody clamped a hand over his mouth and tightened his arms, the words were silenced as his throat was constricted. The man wriggled a few more times, but his brain was shutting down as the air was stopped. He slumped into a coma; the hold was a jujitsu move and would render the thug useless for about twenty or thirty minutes. The second sleeper stirred, but only for a second. As quick as lightning, Gumbao pulled a small leather billy club out of his pocket and whacked the guy across the back of the neck. It was a precise practiced blow. Brody knew his decision had been right, this guy had seen some action. The pirate slumped and was unconscious, back laying on the mat. Brody was impressed. Gumbao looked at him with his toothless grin.

Gumbao muttered, "'Twende.'" 'Let's go.'

So far so good. But the sun would be coming up soon and then their chances diminished considerably. As soon as the birds started their morning chorus and the monkeys began chattering in the trees, there would be life aboard. They had to act fast. Brody checked his Glock for the tenth time. He wanted the rest to surrender, then he could get the girls and get the hell out of there!

The next step in the plan was more difficult and dangerous. Knocking out sleeping men was easy. Dozing armed guards were a completely different ball game. The wooden deck stretched out in front of them, the moon had sunk behind a hill, everything was in shadow before the sun came up. The two men moved silently across the wooden deck. The dhow was old, the planks were worn and loose, and as they crept along the deck creaked and groaned under their feet. Brody could see the two guards still snoozing. There was another guy slumped further back in the cabin, but they could not see the last one.

As they reached midships, a floor hatch flicked open behind them. The two intruders froze, then a warning shout came. The missing pirate had been sleeping below in the small cramped cabin and had obviously been woken by the footsteps on the deck above.

The yell was loud and clear. Brody turned. Before he realized, his training had taken over. The muscle memory, not his brain, took control. He took a knee, at the same time raising his arm. In one swift motion, the trigger was pulled and the bullet fired. The guy took the round right in the mouth. The back of his head came off, splattering blood and brains all over the hatch and deck behind it. The man did not have time to register any shock. The shout of alarm was stopped mid-way as he fell backwards through the hole, making a loud clatter as the dead body tumbled down the steep steps.

That was the first shot. Principle Two now applied. Brody turned just as the first guard was picking up his AK to strafe the forward deck and kill both Brody and Gumbao. He looked right into the guy's dark eyes. The machine gun came up to bear, aiming straight for Brody. He could not react fast enough at this distance with a Glock. Then, from his left, he heard a pinging sound and a flash of silver flew past him. Before he could look or even react, the guard stared down at his chest to see a long silver bolt sticking out. The gun dropped to the floor with a loud clatter. Now, this was going to get more difficult.

Brody ran forward, diving behind a packing case as the bullets started to fly. Gumbao ducked under another crate, then started moving forward in the shadows on the port side of the dhow. Brody came up shooting, firing off five shots. The fusillade forced the guard back further into the cabin. Gumbao had moved along the port side. He stopped his advance to give Brody the chance to catch up. Brody dashed forward getting to the front cabin where the girls were. He was undecided, if he just went for the girls he might bring them out into a full-on firefight, they were probably safer locked up for now. He had to eliminate the threat, then come back for them.

He ran up the stairs. In one quick movement, he rolled onto the upper deck and came up firing. Taking a knee, he sighted on the second guard and shot him three times in the chest, sending him back into the far recesses of the cabin. At that moment, a long rope whipped out of the darkness. The rope had a huge Turk's head knot on the end. It smashed into Brody's hand, knocking the gun free. Brody had a flashback to the original encounter with these guys, the rope and assailant had been his downfall. He rolled to the left as the knot came swinging back, thunking into the deck beside him, leaving a deep gouge in the old wood. He continued rolling across the cabin, moving away from the deadly weapon and the seasoned expert using it.

He managed to get to his feet. The knot whipped past his head again. He ducked as it swooshed over him. The guy in front of him was enjoying himself. He had Brody cornered and knew he could take him whenever he wanted. The rope lashed out and hit Brody in the stomach. The pain was intense, he staggered back, recovering. Brody was concerned. He suddenly realized he could mess this up the second time with the rope. His plan was falling apart.

As the Turk's head came in for a final death blow, Brody caught it about two feet from the end, the thick rope wrapped around his arm the knot hit his forearm with enough force to make him scream in pain.

But now he had the pirate's weapon. Brody was trained in unarmed combat so knew the next few moves would be his. He dove to the floor then spun in a long arc with his foot, catching the guy behind his left knee. The man's leg gave way as he knew it would. Brody took his chance and came up in a crouch, lunging forward and smashing the pirate in the chest with both fists. The thug was knocked backwards, gasping for breath. As Brody rolled back, he jerked the rope out of the staggering pirate's hand.

Now it was his turn. He unwrapped the knot from his arm and started slamming the deck on either side of the big guy, who was edging backwards with fear in his eyes. The pirate was asking for forgiveness, crying out. This guy knew exactly what the Turk's head could do, as he had done it to innocent victims many times in the past. Brody was about to let up and take this guy's surrender, when he was hit on the back of the head with a large piece of wood, like a baseball bat. He went down, but rolled as he was expecting another blow. He was right, it hit the deck inches from his body. Captain Faraj swung the bat again in a large arc, slamming it into the deck next to Brody's head.

Brody rolled again, this time coming up ready. He had two mean-looking brutes ready to kill. He could not see his gun, which would have been handy right now.

Lunging at the captain with the rope was just about keeping him at bay. The other guy was trying to flank him. He swung the knot full force. It caught the thug on the side of his head and he went to his knees again. In a second, the guy was back on his feet and ready. This man was so tough. Brody would never have recovered that fast. With a scream of rage, the pirate charged, Brody saw him coming. And dodged to the side, his hand flicked to the knife on his calf. As the giant passed, he clipped Brody's head, but Brody was faster. He sliced the razor-sharp blade along the inside of the giant's thigh.

The thug ran on into the bulwark, then stood ready for another charge. Brody dodged. The man was slowing down, leaving a trail of thick, dark red blood behind on the planks of the deck. As the pirate was recovering for his third charge, he looked down and could see the large red stain on his torn jeans. The giant's heart was pumping so hard, after all of the exercise. It was not helping him. Brody had sliced the guy's femoral artery; his own heart was pumping him dry. He realized his strength was ebbing. He looked at Brody in disbelief, this man had killed him. His face went white. The guy's heart kept pushing the red liquid around his body until it found the hole in his thigh and pulsed onto the deck. The pirate slumped to his knees then fell face-first on the deck in his own pool of blood.

Brody looked up for a second, readying himself for the blow that would certainly come from Faraj. Instead, he heard a splash as the captain dived overboard. He ran to the gunwale and saw the captain powerfully swimming towards the mangroves a hundred feet away. Damn! He had got away. That was not in the plan.

Brody was bruised and battered, but no mortal wounds. He had just killed three people, which he had vowed never to do again, but it seemed that this was his life. To run away was pointless.

He staggered over to the top rail and looked over the dhow. The two unconscious crew were still oblivious to their fate. The hatch was still open where the pirate had come up to raise the alarm, which had been less than six minutes ago.

Below him, Gumbao had found an iron bar and was breaking the padlock on the girl's cabin. There were screams of fear coming from inside as the girls cried out. Finally, Gumbao broke the lock and the door swung open. Brody had struggled down the steps and was next to Gumbao as they peered into the darkness. The cabin stank of sweat, stale food, and God knows what. In the corner, Brody could just make out a pile of clothes. Gumbao started speaking in Swahili, he said in soothing words, "It's OK. We are here to save you."

They saw a movement in the pile of clothes. The girls had hidden in the corner fearing the worst. One by one, they slowly got to their feet, coming over to the door. Most of the girls looked at Brody like he was some alien. But when Hassan's sister saw him, she ran into his embrace and held on tight. When the girls were on deck, Gumbao and Brody could see they had hardly been fed, their clothes were torn, and they had not been given any place to wash. Mzee and Hassan soon came on board and started assisting the young ladies. The Mzee was instantly helping them cover up, then got some water in a bucket, taking them to the bow to get some privacy so they could clean themselves.

One girl had severe malaria. She looked very pale with a high fever. Brody got his pack from the smaller dhow and gave her his malaria pills. She would soon feel better. Once the girls had been cleaned up a bit, they managed to cover themselves as they felt so exposed without the head to foot covering of the 'buibuis,'. As the morning wore on, their spirits improved. It would take weeks or even months for these young ladies to recover, most had never left the island before.

Brody sat on the end of the gunwale, recovering from the ordeal. It had been close. They could just as easily have lost this fight. Out here no one would have come to the rescue.

Gumbao and Hassan bundled the two guys they had knocked out into a small dingy the dhow carried. They left them with a jerry can of water, shoving them off from the dhow.

Gumbao said, "If I ever hear of you again, see you, or even smell you, then I will use my new speargun on your balls." He continued, "I will come for you and your families, your mothers, your fathers, goats, dogs, and chickens."

The pirates took the message as they floated off. The tide was going out. The dingy would be dragged all the way across the inlet. He was sure the men would manage to untie themselves and escape, then find their way to the mainland.

Brody went below into the tiny cabin. It was filthy. He did not know how the man could have slept here. He stepped over the dead pirate, keeping out of his brains on the floor. He had an ax in his hand from the deck above. He now started at the hull planks, smashing the ax into them time and time again until they began to split.

Once the sea was pouring in, he set about the starboard side below the waterline, smashing away until the ocean was rushing in through the split and broken planks. Then he found the engine in the rear and smashed the seacock which brought the cold water in to cool the motor. The engine room immediately started to flood.

Gumbao had seen what he was doing and had popped into the forward section of the hull and done the same in two places. The dhow was going to sink at anchor.

The inlet was very deep. They could sink the dhow here and it would not be found for many years. The outflow from the mangroves had turned the lagoon a dark tea color with less than five feet of visibility. As soon as the dhow settled on the bottom in the thick mud surrounding the mangrove swamp, no one would know that it was there, even on the off chance someone bothered to come looking. Brody did not want to leave the dhow for Faraj. He was dangerous and could easily come looking for them.

They bundled the three dead guys down with the first one and battened the wooden hatch, some good fish food for the snappers in the area.

As Brody and Gumbao left the stricken dhow, the deck was already awash. She was still anchored and would be held in place, but would disappear from the world as if she had never existed.

They set the girls in the small sleeping cabin and gave them some food and freshwater. They were safe now. The ordeal was over. They would not end up in some Arab's harem, or lost to some militia band of Somalis, or kept as cooks and sex slaves. They could go back to their families and rebuild their lives.

Brody smiled as they pulled the starter on the outboard and headed back out to the open sea. The eclectic team had done it; he had managed to pay a small amount of his debt back to humanity. For once he felt good about himself.

# Epilogue

Brody and his crew set sail into the beautiful morning sunlight. The sea was placid at this time of day, but the life that teemed underneath was already awake. Flying fish were being chased, then flinging themselves out of the water, gliding over the surface for as long as possible, hoping they would not get caught by the predator behind them. Dolphins were swimming alongside the boat, giving the early morning mariners a show of jumping and twisting in the air. The sun slowly rose above the horizon on a new day, an enormous golden orb racing into the sky. The ocean looked as if it was on fire as they sailed along the coast back towards their home.

The dhow sailed on. There was no hurry, no one was chasing them. Hassan taught Brody the art of handlining off the back of a dhow using a long line wrapped around a thick piece of wood, with a jig about three inches in length with two nasty barbed hooks hidden inside. They baited the line and let it out behind the boat about three hundred feet. The jig bounced on the surface as the dhow sailed on. It took about ten minutes. Suddenly, the line went tight in Brody's hand. The piece of wood was almost torn out of his grip as a huge bull dorado leaped out of the ocean, spinning in the air. This was not like rod fishing. There was no brake on the reel, or bend in the rod, just a tug of war between man and fish. Even on a fishing dhow, the rules of engagement applied. You were the fisherman, and you fought the fight, no handing the line over when you were tired. Brody and the dorado battled for over thirty minutes. He slowly wound the line onto the wooden block, foot by excruciating foot. Eventually, he tired the big bull out, and pulled it alongside where Hassan expertly grabbed its gills and tail, lifting it onto the deck. Brody was exhausted from hauling in this massive fish. It must have weighed 45 pounds. He was hooked though. This was man against nature with nothing in between, just the way he liked it.

They were heading into the south-easterly wind. The little dhow had to tack to make any headway. Each day, as soon as the wind came up around 09:30, the crew would pull the boom up to the top of the mast, setting the sail. They ran at forty-five degrees to the wind, sailing as close as they could, keeping the sails filled. When the coast was long gone over the horizon to the west after about four hours sailing, they would tack the little boat and head back to shore.

Brody was keen to learn. He marvelled at the way Hassan expertly hopped around the bow as it was lunging up and down in the swell of the waves. He convinced Hassan to let him have a go. After much argument and discussions on which was the best way forward, the rest of the crew agreed. Brody was trained in the art of dhow tacking. On his first attempt, they were very easy on him. In a light wind with no swell, they tacked. His natural ability and strength carried him through.

Later in the day, he insisted on doing the second tack: this was much rougher as the wind was up and they were a long way out to sea. Brody managed to fight with the sail to bring it into the boom, then pulled it tight, and wrapped the sheet around his arm as he had been taught. He started rolling the boom around the masthead with his feet on the tip of the bow. Suddenly, a large wave came taking, the bow up and dropping it like a stone. Brody screamed as the world turned upside down. The boat had disappeared from under his feet. He was plunged into the cold water, head first, then dragged along the side of the craft. Luckily the sheet was still wrapped around his arm. Hassan and Gumbao pulled the rope back aboard with Brody attached. He lay gasping and coughing saltwater onto the deck, getting his breath back. Mzee and Gumbao chuckled to each other.

Mzee said as he laughed, "Too fast, my friend, you must learn to walk first, you are only a child out here!"

They zigzagged like this all the way down the coast. Brody had a feeling he needed some space. These guys were great, but he needed to get his head straight.

The girls were reticent, mostly keeping themselves to themselves. They ate, slept, and prayed. It would take a long time for them to get over the ordeal. Swahili girls did not spend much time on boats as it was men's work. The small dhow was an alien place for them and very uncomfortable. However, they made the best of it, learning to live on the deck with the crew, slowly adapting to this new way of life. But old habits die hard. They kept covered from head to foot, at all times, it was only Hassan's sister that would talk to Brody. She was hungry for knowledge, wanting to learn as much English as possible. Brody could see she had a quick and intelligent mind and would go far. He taught her as much as he could, dragging up the memories of the English they had beaten into him when he had attempted school all those years ago.

As they passed Mombasa harbor, Brody knew he would not be going all the way back with them this time. He made up an excuse for Hassan that some business had come up which needed his attention. However, as soon as it was over, he would come back to the island and continue his scuba diving.

The dhow pulled in at Shimoni, the last point of Kenya. Brody shook hands with the old Mzee and Gumba. Hassan hugged him along with all of the girls. Everyone begged him to sail across the channel to Pemba, where they would have a massive homecoming party. But Brody politely refused. He needed to get some time alone. His new friends were great, but his past still haunted him. Too much company was more than he could handle right now, and a party would just make it worse.

He jumped off the dhow onto the beach in the quiet village of Shimoni. This was a one-horse town if ever there was one. He wandered along the broken path of the main street. It was silent, just a few goats and chickens looking for some morsels to eat. Shimoni had once been a major slave trading port. There were caves beneath the road with the original shackles still attached to the walls. The caves had held the captive slaves before they were hoarded onto the ships to be taken to Zanzibar or north past the Horn of Africa never to be seen again.

It was a bit depressing. But Brody needed a rest, to recover, and most of all a drink. He headed down the lane towards the lights. A big, black metal gate on the side of the road displaying a hotel sign, beckoned to him. The guard let Brody in, looking at him strangely. He only carried a seabag and was walking, no vehicle.

The guard tactfully asked, "You came without your car, sir?"

Brody laughed and said, "Do you have a bar at this place?"

The guard pointed and a few minutes later Brody was sat on a bar stool with a double, single malt whiskey in his hand. He knew this would not be the last tonight.

The End

Dear Reader,

I sincerely hope you enjoyed this story as much as I have enjoyed writing it. The East African coast has been my home now for nearly twenty years and I love it as much as Brody does. All the locations are based on actual places and islands; they can easily be found on Google Earth. The people in the story are fictitious, but they are based on people I know and have met over the years.

If you did enjoy the read, or in fact, if you didn't, I would very much appreciate some feedback on this book's page. Just type in the title on Amazon Kindle and let me know what you think. Good or bad, I am always interested as the reviews make me a better writer for the future. I would also appreciate it if you could put me on twitter or any other book sites where you think readers would enjoy this story.

Alternatively, my email is steve@stevebrakerbooks.com. I would love to hear from you, and I answer all of the emails personally.

I am now sat with Brody as he gets ready for his next tropical adventure, I am sure if you enjoyed the first book you will enjoy the second. As I am getting to know Brody as a character and his thought process, the stories become more involved, and I hope more enjoyable for you. This series will go on as long as he has interesting stories to tell.

I consider myself very lucky to have lived in East Africa for so long. I have traveled up and down this coastline fishing, diving, and exploring. Most of the descriptions are based on my actual experiences here. This I think puts me in a unique position to be able to give you the best and most realistic view on life in East Africa.

Brody's second instalment, 'African Treasure,' is out now and available through Kindle and Kindle paperback. I hope you enjoy them and continue following Brody and his adventures.

If you would like to sign up for my newsletter, then please click on this link, it will take you to our sign-up page. We don't send out loads of emails, just important stuff like book launches. We also keep your address personal to us www.stevebrakerbooks.com we also have a website which you can visit if you would like at http://www.stevebrakerbooks.com. I would be happy to welcome you to my Facebook page which is https://www.facebook.com/AfricanOceanAdventures/.

I hope to see you soon. Happy adventures!

Yours,


Steve Braker

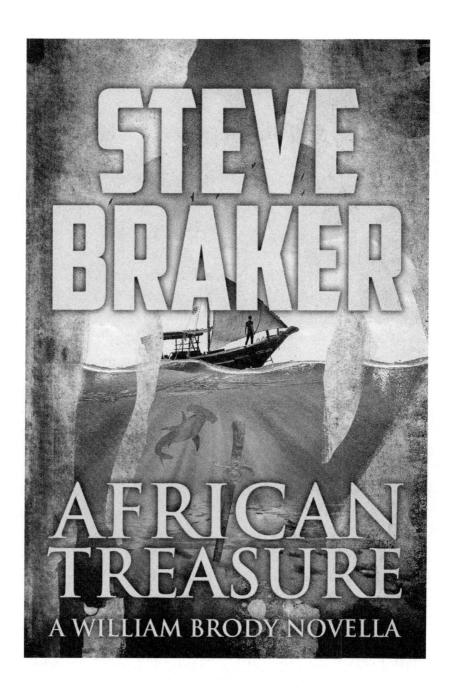

**Excerpt from Book Two. African Treasure**

# Chapter One

---

# The Anstel

Captain William Murray climbed the steps from the main deck to the quarter deck. The wind was whistling through his blond, thinning hair and whipped at the long seaman jacket attempting to keep him warm. A pair of worn leather, sea boots, molded to his feet through many years of wear and repair, adorned his feet planting him firmly on the wooden deck. He could feel the swell of the ocean as if he was standing on the surface. Captain Murray was now fifty-one years of age. An old captain, he knew this game was for the youngsters, but since his wife had died of pleurisy five years ago, he had not even bothered with shore leave. The Captain lived a spartan life on board the ship he adored. She was named the 'Anstel,'. Which would be his home now for as long as the company would agree for him to sail her. Eight bells had just been rung on the lovely bronze ship's bell. He loved the bell. It made him feel at home, like the peal of the parish church bells in his childhood village. He could recognize the clear chime over any other bell on any other ship. Every one of the British East Indian Company ships had such a bell, and each one was proudly engraved with the ship's name and B.E.I.C., British East India Company.

Captain Murray was a stickler for shipshape and seaman fashion. The deck was always holystoned, the ship's bell was polished so brightly it gleamed in the moonlight. Ropes and lines were ready or stowed neatly in the rope lockers. This was a company ship and had to represent the company.

The captain had made it a personal rule to come on deck around this time each night. He would make his rounds, ensuring everyone stayed alert during the early hours of the new day. Many ships had become stricken or sunk due to the watch being asleep at 04:00 hours. He walked the deck, chatting with the keen-eyed lookouts, making sure none were dozing. The crew knew and liked the captain. He had been on the *Anstel* for over 10 years, plying the British East Indian routes across the globe. Captain Murray and his First Mate James Tamworth, a Southerner from the famous city of Plymouth, were good to the crew. James's father had been a seaman for the Royal Navy. But as there was peace now, James had opted to work for the British East India Company and be sent all over the world to trade with other nations.

The moon shone brightly above them, showing the large, long swells of the Indian Ocean coming in from the south. The sky was very dark on the horizon. Massive storm clouds had been brewing and jostling for position since early yesterday afternoon. There was going to be a blow, he knew it. Just how bad? Captain Murray had been on the seaman and boy, so knew the ocean was a cruel mistress. She could be all placid or playful, then, just like his late wife, in the split of an eye, she could be a vengeful mistress beating you with all she had, without mercy. If you survived, then it was more luck than judgment. Many of his friends had gone to the deep over the years, and he had come close too often to count.

The year was 1858, a good year for Captain Murray. He had sailed the whole year, usually from London East India Docks across to West Africa and then back. This last trip had been different; he had been sent all the way to the East Coast of India, a perilous journey even in this modern age of the compass and celestial navigation. The *Anstel* had crossed the channel then sailed along the West Coast of Africa until reaching the Cape. Then, after battling his way through some of the roughest water in the world, he had beat back up the East Coast of Africa until he came to the port of Mombasa then onwards along the coast until they were some two hundred miles from the Horn. Then they turned East to cross the Indian Ocean. As long as the Captain knew which line of latitude he started on and maintained a steady course, they would find their way. The alternative was crossing from Madagascar and then to Seychelles. This was a tough call. Madagascar was fine as it was so big you could usually site it after a day or two off the coast of East Africa. But then finding the Seychelles was a different kettle of fish altogether. The tiny group of atolls were spread out over five hundred miles in the middle of a huge ocean. With some bad weather or lazy seamanship, it was easy to miss them completely, sail right past them. Then he would have to dead reckon all the way to Sri-Lanka, if he was lucky. The Maldives were treacherous, full of reefs and tiny islands hidden off the coast of Sri Lanka. These coral reefs and islands could be just under the surface and easily tear the hull out of his beautiful ship. It had happened to many competent captains before him, rushing for Madras.

He had heard of the carpenter in England who had come up with the wooden clock to solve all of their problems. No one could tell where the longitude was, it was impossible to find accurately. James and William would discuss at length the celestial readings and argue left and right as to exactly where they were. John Harrison's Marine Chronometer was just becoming available, but it was so expensive he doubted he would ever see such a thing on one of his ships. So it was dead reckoning and celestial navigation for them. This was the reason most captains hugged the coasts then made a dash in as straight a line as possible across the unforgiving ocean.

The ship had made Madras without any trouble; his one-hundred-man crew had worked together well. Captain Murray kept his men fed and watered, always carrying enough rum to keep them happy while off watch. The bosun had hauled the sails, keeping them as trim as possible, making excellent way across the Indian Ocean.

Once the *Anstel* had docked, Captain Murray reported to Sir Harry Donaldson, the director in charge of British East India Company Assets there. He was a portly man in his early fifties with a keen smile, standing at least six foot three inches in stocking feet. Sir Harry loved to ride and hunt, he kept a stable of some fifteen thoroughbred horses. His beautiful mansion was adorned with the heads of all the unlucky animals he had encountered on his hunting expeditions. In the study was an enormous black and orange rug in front of the fire. It was a huge Bengali tiger he had shot some years ago. Its canines were at least four inches long.

Sir Harry was big in every way; his massive barrel chest would heave as he laughed like a bass drum. He was quick-witted and loved his job. It seemed he loved India too. They had spent a good deal of time together while Captain Murray was in the city. The East India Company had taken over Madras nearly one hundred years earlier. They had used the fortress city ever since, exporting fine cloth, spices, and of course tea, along with a lot of loot removed from the defeated Raj.

When they had arrived in Madras, all the news had been about the mutiny. The Indian Regiments known as the Sepoys had risen up against their oppressors, the British.

Sir Harry explained, "The Sepoys are a tough bunch, mostly thieves and scallywags. Their only life is the army, and they have been oppressed for many years."

He seemed to have a certain amount of empathy for their feelings.

He went on, "Generally, the Sepoy has a tough life. He is the lowest of the low in the army and can never attain any full rank. These poor buggers are always sent on dangerous missions and have to put up with substandard equipment, pay, and food."

The gossip in Madras City markets was the mutiny had occurred because the army had changed the charges for the muskets. When a soldier loaded his musket, he had to tear the top of the paper charge off with his teeth, as he was holding the weapon in one hand and the ramrod in the other. This caused discontent as the Sepoy believed the new charges were dipped in pork fat to keep the powder dry. A taboo in most vegetarian Indian cultures. Another reason was bad food. The Sepoy were not allowed to take their wives on campaigns, so they had to eat what the army offered, which was often not very good fare. The Sepoy was an Indian and needed his curries and spices.

There were many reasons, but the up of it all was they had mutinied on the 10th of May the previous year and had now taken Delhi and crowned a new Raj of India. This was not good news and was very worrying for all the British East Indian Company personnel.

Sir Harry said, "I am not leaving this place. My wife Isabell and I have lived here for nearly 30 years. It is our home. In fact, it is more a home to us than England. We would be strangers there now. Most of my pals died in the war anyway."

Sir Harry went on, red-faced, thoughtfully puffing on his cigar, "Anyway, what is left for me in England? I hardly know the place anymore. I have not been back to London for nearly twelve years. Even the food now would disagree with me and with the bloody cold, my gout would play up something awful." After looking Captain Murray in the eye with a glint and a wink, Sir Harry went on, "The Company rarely bothers me here as long as the ships are full and I make the shareholders rich. This place is mine, like a king I am. Great life; couldn't beat it." With that, he finished the conversation and led Captain Murray to the study for some more brandy. Captain Murray had to agree Sir Harry had a pretty good life here.

James and the crew worked hard day and night loading the *Anstel*. She was built for this work. An Indiaman, she was 146 feet and 9 inches from stem to stern, weighing in at 820 tons, made of good English oak. She sailed well with her 100-man crew and two officers. She had three decks and could run out 26 guns if required. These had mostly been removed by the company since the war, and now the seas were even free from most pirates, so they only carried 12 cannons, giving them more hold space for expensive goods and chattels.

The hold gradually filled with crate upon crate of precious tea, then fine linens and cloth, and finally the barrels of wonderfully smelling spices. The aromas of coriander, turmeric, cardamom, and tamarind filled the ship. It smelled like an Indian bazaar. They were making ready to sail on the following morning tide when Sir Harry came down to the wharf and invited Captain Murry up for a final dinner. Murray was glad of the chance. He faced a five-thousand-mile journey ahead of him, and home cooking was not going to be on the menu once they set sail in the morning.

The farewell meal was fantastic. Sir Harry was on form, and his beautiful wife Isabell had arranged for some exquisite Indian delicacies. They had red snapper from the creek, then samosas, small pastry envelopes of curried goat or dhal deep-fried, followed by roast suckling pig with local vegetables. It was a delicious meal, all served along with fine wines matching superbly with each course. As usual, Sir Harry was the center of attention, telling them hunting stories, keeping everyone entertained throughout the evening.

As the dessert was served, good old English apple pie with custard, Sir Harry tapped his glass to get some quiet, "Thanks to my beautiful wife Isabell for this sumptuous meal all organized by her fair hand. The garden is her domain too."

He then called for the chef from the kitchen.

Sir Harry said, "Sir, this is a splendid meal. Your skills in the kitchen are second to none. I commend you on such a wonderfully prepared meal, I toast you and my wife, and I hope for many more like it."

The old rascal then coughed. As was the way of English gentry at this time of the meal, the gentlemen adjourned to the library for brandy and cigars, and to discuss the final details before Captain Murry set sail.

Sir Harry asked, "Captain, I need you to take on board some accounting books and letters for the Company. There are a few trinkets too. I have to keep them happy in Blighty, or they will come and see me, God forbid!".

Sir Harry then became somber, he said. "Look here, Murray, this mutiny is damned awful. I am hearing grumbles in my own troops, you know, and I treat them damned well." Murray was not sure what to say.

Sir Harry carried on, "This business could be a rum turn for us all. We are outnumbered thousands to one on this continent. If the Sepoys decided to chuck us all out, then so be it." Sir Harry took a long pull on his cigar then swallowed a whole glass of Napoleon brandy.

He said, "I have decided the best thing is to empty the safe and get all the loot that the Company has here back to London for safekeeping. I can see you are a trustworthy gentleman with many years' experience with the Company, so I am entrusting it to you."

That was the end of it. Murray accepted, of course. He worked for the East India Company; he had no choice really.

The following morning before sunrise, a troop of Sepoy arrived at the *Anstel* with a horse and cart. There were five large sea chests piled high on the back. The Indian soldiers manhandled them to the quayside. The bosun arranged a block and tackle to winch the sea chests aboard they were so heavy. Captain Murray, good to his word, stowed them in his captain's cabin, which was the safest place on the ship.

Sir Harry and Isabell came to wave them off as they set sail back home. The Anstel traveled down the East Coast of India then out into the Indian Ocean. At the tip of Sri Lanka, on the 7 degrees' latitude mark, Captain Murray altered course and turned due west, heading for the coast of Africa. His plan was to arrive somewhere near Mombasa; they could then sail south to the Cape and continue home.

You can get this great book by going to this link on my web site https://www.stevebrakerbooks.com/african-treasure/. Or alternatively, head back to Amazon Kindle and type into the search bar 'Steve Braker African Treasure.'

# Copyright

This is a work of fiction. Names, characters, and incidents are either the products of the author's imagination or are used fictitiously and any resemblance to persons, living or dead, businesses, companies, events, is entirely coincidental.

The locations and distances are real, the Island of Pemba I have visited and dived on many times. The village is a typical village on the East African Coast but is fictitious, made from many visits I have made to many villages.

Pirates are of course fictitious, but the area is still known for occasional disappearances of young girls and boys. The child soldiers are a serious problem all over Africa and a real social problem to be dealt with.

Copyright © 2017

All rights reserved

Printed in Great Britain
by Amazon

38723702R00076